Hardcourt Upset

*Chip's reaction was a replica of a lightning
pass on a football field*

A CHIP HILTON SPORTS STORY

Hardcourt Upset

BY CLAIR BEE

GROSSET & DUNLAP   *Publishers*   New York

Contents

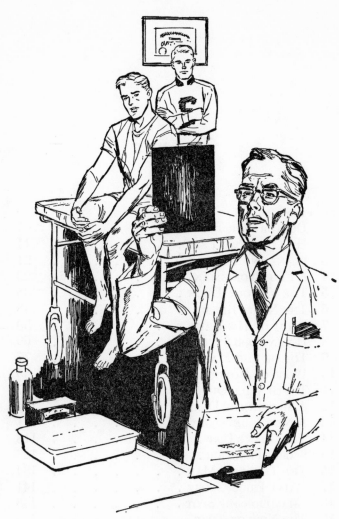

Dr. Terring held the X ray up to the light

CHAPTER 1

DOCTOR'S ORDERS

DR. MIKE TERRING, State's team physician, was examining Chip Hilton's injured knee. He lifted the varsity star's leg, straightened it out, and with his fingers pressed the knee here and there. While doing this, he posed the same questions over and over: "Hurt? . . . No? . . . How about this? . . ."

Chip wiped his moist brow with the back of his hand and shook his head. "No, Doc, just hurts a little when I bend my leg."

Dr. Terring carried a sheaf of X rays over to the window in the front of the office. He held each print up to the light and scrutinized it with minute care.

Chip was perched on the end of the examining table, rocking nervously back and forth, holding his right knee between the long fingers of his locked hands. It was cool in the room but small beads of perspiration covered his forehead. Beside the table, Soapy Smith, Chip's lifelong friend, shifted restlessly from one foot to the other and watched the physician with anxious eyes.

Dr. Terring appeared to be satisfied at last and

1

walked back to the table. He tossed the X rays on his desk and hooked his thumbs in the armholes of his vest. "Well, Chip, there's nothing broken or chipped. But the ligament is swollen badly."

"Then it isn't the cartilage?"

"Nope! Strained ligament. It can be pretty painful."

"I don't mind the pain."

Dr. Terring peered over his glasses and grinned. "No? Well, my boy, if you use this knee for basketball you'll take that back. You've got to cut out the running."

"In other words, no basketball."

The physician nodded. "That's right."

"But I've got to play, Doc. We've got a chance to win the conference. Maybe the N.C.A.A."

"Got to defend his marksmanship title, too," Soapy added.

Dr. Terring grunted and studied the knee again, pressing gently on the joint. "I know, I know," he said testily, "but I don't like it. Shooting around a little might help, providing you got enough rest. But running and jumping and turning—no!"

Chip gripped the table fiercely. "But couldn't I be careful of it when I play, Doc? It doesn't hurt very much."

"Doesn't hurt, eh? Is that so? Well, let's see." Terring grasped the knee again. "All right here? Here? And here? But how about this?" He pressed the side of the knee sharply and watched Chip's reaction.

Chip winced despite his efforts to conceal the pain. "Ummm . . ." he grunted.

"That's what I was getting at," the doctor said dryly.

"But that's different from running," Soapy protested, placing a hand on Chip's shoulder.

"Not much different," Terring said shortly. He studied Chip for a second and then continued slowly, "You athletes are all alike. Always in a hurry. Afraid you'll miss a practice or a game. Lots of kids ruin fine sports careers just because they're impatient, won't give an injury enough rest. . . .

"Why, I've seen kids cripple their arms for life by throwing a baseball from the centerfield fence clear to home plate without warming up, or show off in football by tackling without a helmet. And," he added significantly, "I know of certain cases where a boy made the mistake of using a bum leg when the doctor told him to lay off. . . .

"Another thing! Don't you let any of this hero stuff run away with you. It's good to win championships, but not at the expense of your health. Besides, you've got two big years left. Seems to me you've done pretty good for a sophomore. All-America quarterback in football and Most Valuable Player in the basketball tournament."

"But, Doc, you don't understand! I can't run out on the team."

"You mean *walk* out," Dr. Terring contradicted grimly. He paused and then said gently, "I don't want to scare you, Chip, but a strained ligament can be disastrous."

Dr. Terring walked over to a closet. Opening the door, he pulled out an old brace and shook it in the air. "It's a little old and beat up, Chipper, but it will do. Now you wear this until we can get you a new one."

Under the physician's watchful eyes, Chip strapped the brace on his knee. Then, while he was pulling on his trousers, Dr. Terring continued, "A knee is a tricky animal, Chip. This one needs analgesic packs, heat, whirlpool treatments, diathermy —and a vacation."

"How much of a vacation, sir?"

"Oh, a week or ten days."

"But I can't miss that much basketball."

"I'm afraid you will have to, Hilton. Let's put it this way. Today is the third of January. Semester exams begin in a couple of weeks, with the big part of the basketball season coming up in February. Isn't it important that you be in good shape for the stretch drive? Isn't it better to miss three or four games now than to miss the entire season?"

"I'm sure of that, sir. It's just that I'd like to play."

"I know. But a week or so won't ruin the whole season."

Chip shook his head uncertainly. "I guess not," he said ruefully. "I probably wouldn't be much good, anyway. Shall I keep wearing the brace?"

"Absolutely. And no practice of any kind."

Dr. Terring turned back to his desk and Chip and Soapy walked slowly out of the office and along the hall toward the street. Down below, in the gym, pounding feet and joyous shouts reminded the two boys that State's varsity basketball team was busily at work.

"A week!" Chip groaned.

"Maybe more," Soapy added glumly.

Chip reached for the knob of the street door but Soapy brushed past him and shouldered it open. An icy gust of wind and snow greeted the redhead and he caught his breath. "Wow!" he cried, pushing Chip back. "You stay here. I'll see if I can find someone to drive us to work."

Before he could protest, Soapy was gone. Chip shivered and walked slowly away from the door, feeling the cold air bite through his topcoat. Before he reached the trophy cases lining the wall, Soapy was back.

"C'mon, Chip, hurry! Got a lift! Right to the store."

Chip hurried after his pal, hunching his shoulders against the wind. Inside the car, he breathed a sigh of relief. "Pretty cold," he ventured.

"Say that again," the stranger replied.

"We sure appreciate the ride," Soapy said earnestly. "Not many cars out on a day like this."

"No trouble," the driver said, eying Chip in the mirror. "Say, you're Chip Hilton, aren't you?"

"Yes, I am."

"Been readin' about that knee of yours in the paper. How soon you gonna be back in the line-up?"

That was enough for Soapy. He took over, detailing the part Chip had played in State's triumphant march to the championship in the Holiday Invitational Tournament. Chip breathed a sigh of relief when the stranger halted the car in front of State Drug and let them out.

Just outside the store, on Main Street, Chip and Soapy paused and viewed the interior through the window. Fireball Finley and Whitty Whittemore were serving customers at the fountain. Just inside the door, Soapy's hopeless crush, petite Mitzi Savrill was making change for a customer. Chip grinned happily and opened the door.

Mitzi saw Chip first. "And thirty makes— Chip! What did the doctor say about your knee?"

"Nothing much, Mitzi."

Fireball and Whitty almost bumped heads as they

turned. "Well whaddaya know?" Fireball cried. "We've got important company."

"The tall guy with the blond hair looks familiar," Whitty added. "Hey, wait! I know *him!* That's Chip Hilton!"

"The redhead talking to the cashier drops in here a lot," Fireball added. "I think he's got a case on her."

"You can say that again!" Soapy retorted.

"They probably dropped in for a visit," Fireball suggested. He watched Chip walk toward the stockroom. "How's the leg, Chipper?" he asked soberly. "All right?"

"Pretty good, Fireball. Where's Eddie?"

Finley nodded toward the rear of the store. "Stockroom."

"Meet you in Pete's after work," Whitty called. "O.K.?"

Chip nodded assent and went on to the stockroom. Inside, he found Eddie Redding and Mr. George Grayson, owner of State Drug.

"What's the verdict, Chip?" Mr. Grayson asked.

"Dr. Terring said I can't play for a week or so."

"What about working, walking around?"

"Walking is all right. But I can't practice."

"I can use you as a relief cashier, Chip. You give the word."

"Oh, no, Mr. Grayson. My knee is all right. It's just the running and turning in basketball."

"All right, but take it easy."

Chip devoted the rest of the evening to clearing up the back orders which had piled up during the Christmas holidays. He was dead tired when Soapy, Fireball, and Whitty barged in and peeled off their fountain coats.

"Come on!" Fireball urged. "I'm starving."

Pete's Place was only a few steps from State Drug but it seemed a mile to Chip. The little restaurant was crowded when the four State Drug pals filed in and headed for a booth opposite the counter. Jimmy Lu Chung and Pete, the owner, hailed Chip and hurried over to the table. "Hiya, Chip," Jimmy said, gripping his friend's hand eagerly. "How's the leg?"

"All right, I guess. When did you get back?"

"This morning. Grandpop and Pop and Tommy send regards."

"You gonna play Wednesday night?" Pete asked.

Chip shook his head. "Dr. Terring put me on the ex-athletics list."

"Well, anyway, we're all glad you're walking around under your own steam. Wow! We're gettin' jammed up. Take care of these guys, Jimmy. I'll get the counter."

The four boys took a long time eating their sandwiches. The restaurant was warm and cozy and the conversation interesting.

"I like it here," Whitty said drowsily. "Too bad we can't stay all night."

"Well, we can't," Chip said decisively. "Let's hit the road."

"Nothing doing!" Soapy protested. "I'm going to call a cab."

A few minutes later a taxi appeared to take them to the dormitory. Chip and Soapy wasted little time getting upstairs to their room and into bed.

The next morning Soapy was the first to awaken. Chip was breathing heavily in deep sleep and Soapy dressed quietly. He tiptoed out of the room and hurried down the flight of steps to the first floor. Jeff's residents were just beginning to come to life when Soapy opened the front door and headed for the corner newsstand. But when he returned, the dormitory was buzzing with frenzied action.

Soapy ran upstairs and shook Chip until his eyes blinked open. "O.K., Chipper. Hit the deck."

While Chip was dressing, Soapy rustled through the sports pages of the *News* to see what it had to say about the coming game with Tech. "Hey, Chip!" he said, tapping the paper excitedly. "Listen to this guy Locke. He's at it again. Listen! 'State should restrict its competition to schools in its own class.' How about that? This Locke never gets tired, does he?"

"He's got to write something, Soapy. You can't fill up a sports section with scores and statistics."

"Sure, Chip, but it shouldn't be filled up with a lot of half-truths and innu—" Soapy spread his hands and shrugged. "Well, with stuff like that. . . . You better hurry. Hey! You're limping bad! Your leg all right?"

Chip nodded. "Sure, Soapy. It's always stiff in the morning. It will loosen up as soon as I do a little walking. I'm ready. Let's go."

Tuesday was one of Chip's busiest schooldays. Each class seemed to carry him to the most distant building on the campus. He had never noticed the long treks before. In fact, he had welcomed the outdoor breaks and the fresh air. But not today. His knee stiffened up during the lectures and the brace added to his discomfort.

The knee wasn't the only annoyance. The students were in a festive mood, talking about the happenings at home during their year-end vacation—dates, dances, travel experiences. But they weren't over-looking Chip's part in the holiday basketball tournament at Clinton. They surrounded him at every opportunity.

"Nice going, Hilton! You guys fooled every expert in the country."

"Don't know how you guys did it."

"It was simple. They didn't lose any games."

"Wise guy!"

"You shouldn't be walking around so much. The guy that laid out this campus must've been a marathon runner."

"See you at the rally tonight. Better get your speech ready."

Chip tried to be pleasant with everyone, but it was a task. And that afternoon, his science lab period seemed to last forever. He was on his feet during most of the two-hour period, and when it ended, he had a strong inclination to head for Jeff. But he shrugged off the thought and started the hike across the campus to Alumni Gym, stopping from time to time to rest. At last he reached the building and opened the door of Murph Kelly's training quarters.

Kelly worked on Chip's knee for the next half hour, then led the way to the gym and up in the bleachers to watch the varsity practice. As they watched, the veteran trainer kept up a running commentary about the players.

"Chip, this team is the ninth wonder of the world. But take 'em individually, with a couple of exceptions, they're just a bunch of ordinary ball-players. Now take the seniors, Markley, Thornhill, and Gowdy. Heck, they're run of the mill." He patted Chip's arm. "Don't get me wrong, Chip, they're nice fellows. But championship ballplayers? Uh, uh."

"But they won the tournament, Murph."

"Sure they did. But they had a bunch of upsets going for them, plus a lot of spirit and drive and some breaks. Chip, you know as well as I do that Southwestern is the best team in the country. We caught 'em by surprise with the zone press."

"But how about Dane and Southeastern and Templeton?"

Kelly continued on as if he hadn't heard Chip. "The juniors on the squad—King, Di Santis, Tucker, and Lu Chung—well, they can be classed as fair reserves. Period!"

Chip shook his head vigorously. "You're wrong about Jimmy. He's great! He's the best dribbler I ever saw."

Kelly nodded agreement. "You're absolutely right. The best dribbler *anyone* ever saw. . . .

"Then we come to your group. The sophomores. The number one player in that group is Chip Hilton. And they don't come any better."

Chip gave Kelly a friendly shove. "Hey! Stop!"

"The rest of the sophomores," Kelly continued imperturbably, "Morris, Reardon, and Bollinger, have possibilities. Especially Bollinger. The big fellow was a conceited jerk last year. Had to be a ballplayer, though. Six-nine in his stocking feet and fast. And with a father who drummed round ball at him for nineteen years. Yep, had to be. The big guy has come a long way in spite of his old man."

Kelly grinned and nudged Chip. "Guess you think I'm disloyal to the team. Not so! Just been looking at basketball too long to classify this team as anything but lucky!"

CHAPTER 2

HIS OWN TWO FEET

CHIP didn't feel much like working that night, but he wasn't ready to accept his boss's offer of a chair job. A fellow stood on his own two feet, good or bad, when he accepted the responsibilities of a tough job. And the stockroom job was tough! That night Chip and his assistant kept going until nine o'clock. Then Eddie left for home and Chip wearily dropped down in the chair beside the desk. He scarcely looked up when Soapy came swinging through the door.

"You should've seen it, Chip. It was great! There must have been a thousand boxes on the bonfire. Lit up the whole campus. About everyone in school was there, I guess. . . .

"Had the team up on a platform and Prexy Babcock made a speech and said the school was proud of the team and he congratulated everyone and then the cheerleaders and the band took over."

"The band?"

"Sure! They played the Alma Mater and the cheerleaders led some cheers and then Corrigan and all the players made speeches. You should've heard—"

11

"You mean Speed, Sky, and Jimmy made speeches?"

"Well, Speed and Bollinger didn't say much, but Jimmy was great. Corrigan introduced all the guys real nice, but when Jimmy stood up, the crowd cheered him for about five minutes. He didn't need an introduction."

"What did he say?"

"Nothing much. Just said *you* won the tournament."

"*I* won the tournament! Oh, *no!*"

"Oh, *yes!* He said State couldn't have made it to the finals if it hadn't been for your playing and that he wouldn't even have been in the championship game if you hadn't talked his father into letting him come back to school."

"He shouldn't have said that."

"Why not? It's true! Anyway, the crowd began hollering for you, and Corrigan said you had been excused because of your knee but that you would be all right in a few days. I hope, I hope . . ."

"Me, too," Chip said grimly.

"Oh, yes, Chip. I forgot. Just before it broke up, a bunch of Tech fellows drove up in a big truck with a loud-speaker, made some speeches and played some Tech songs. They were bragging about seven straight and they had a little lyric about State bein' number eight. It wasn't bad.

"Then some of our guys began wondering what the truck would look like upside down and you should've seen those Tech guys high-tail it out of there. Some fun! Well, back to the mines. Oh, by the way, Mitzi said I could use her car."

"What for?"

"To take you home after work."

"Take *me* home?"

Soapy grinned delightedly. "Sure! It works out great. I drive you home and come back for Mitzi. Every night! We get through at ten thirty and she's never finished before eleven or eleven fifteen. We'll even have time for a fast sandwich."

"How do *you* get home?"

"She drops me off on her way home."

Chip shook his head. "Nothing doing. I'll walk."

"Gee, Chip, you know I hardly ever get to see Mitzi except when she's working."

Chip grinned. "I thought you were worried about my knee."

Soapy's face reddened. "I am, Chip, I am. But . . ."

"I see," Chip said, pausing to enjoy his pal's embarrassment.

"Aw, Chip, you know how I feel about Mitzi."

Chip nodded. "Sure. Sure, I know."

"Then it's O.K.?"

"I guess it has to be."

Soapy grinned happily and bolted for the door. "O.K. Then we'll start tonight. See you later."

Pete's Place was unusually quiet when the State Drug crowd arrived for their after-work snack that night. Pete took the orders and Jimmy Lu Chung joined them in the booth.

"Hear you made a speech, Jimmy," Chip said. "What's the big idea?"

"Speech? Idea?" Jimmy echoed. "Oh, sure, everybody made a speech. You know something," he said, changing the subject. "I'm worried about the game tomorrow night."

"You'll kill 'em," Soapy said with a grimace.

"And how!" Fireball added. "So Tech has won

seven games straight— What teams did they beat?"

"They beat Southern," Whittemore said. "That's more than we could do."

"Sure," Fireball agreed, "but that was the first game of the season and Chip wasn't playing."

"Chip won't be playing tomorrow night, either," Soapy added dourly.

"Tech must have something," Chip said reflectively. "It isn't very smart to underestimate *any* team."

"Well, playing on the home court is worth ten points," Soapy said. "That ought to help. Oh, oh, we've gotta go, Chip. Getting late. Car is outside."

"Car?" Fireball echoed. "What car? Where you goin'?"

"Mitzi's car," Soapy whispered mysteriously. "I'll tell you all about it sometime. All I can say now is that she is sending me on an important mission every night."

"I'll bet," Fireball said.

"It's true," Soapy said. "You guys wanta go home, too?"

"Not us," Whitty said, glancing at the clock. "We went through that eleven-o'clock business all through football. Remember?"

Game tension began building up in Chip early the next morning. It was difficult to concentrate in his classes and later that afternoon at work. He and Soapy had a quick hamburger at Pete's Place at six o'clock and started out for the game. It was only seven o'clock when they reached Alumni Gym, but the crowd was already moving toward the entrance. Cars were parked in long rows along every street and the parking lots on each side of the gym were filling up rapidly. Here and there in the crowd, Tech rooters carried pennants and talked loudly about their undefeated team.

"We should have been invited to the tournament."

"Yeah, seven in a row and we weren't good enough. Guess our school is too small."

"Our team's big. What's the size of the school got to do with it?"

"Everything! Besides, a team has got to have *names*. We don't have any big names on our team."

"But we've got a *team*. And we're undefeated."

"Sure! Uninvited, too!"

Soapy glanced resignedly at Chip as they reached the locker room. Chip stopped with his hand on the doorknob, listening to the banging of lockers and Murph Kelly's growling orders. Suddenly he turned. "Come on! I'll sit with you."

"But you're supposed to be on the bench."

"No, I'm not. I'd be in the way. We'll sit up behind the north basket. Best seat in the house."

"Right!"

They followed the fans slowly up the steps and gained seats high above the floor. Down below, the shining court looked like a glossy caramel.

Chip glanced at the scoreboard. State's freshmen were giving the Tech neophytes a bad licking. With a little over a minute left to play, the junior Statesmen were leading, 71 to 34. The words of the Tech rooters came to mind. Chip guessed they were right—there sure didn't seem to be any big-name stars playing on Tech's frosh team.

The preliminary game ended then and the Tech varsity came trotting out. A burst of applause greeted them but it was overwhelmed by the resounding roar which exploded as State's white-clad varsity dashed on the court. Chip's heart jumped and he found himself on his feet beside Soapy cheering for his teammates. He was so engrossed in watching Jimmy, Speed, Sky, Bitsy, Rud Slater and the veterans dash through the warm-up drills that he didn't realize he was still standing after the neighboring fans had taken their seats.

Soapy tugged at his coat. "Chip! Sit down."

Chip glanced around sheepishly and sat down, still applauding. Then he concentrated on the Tech squad. The Engineers were small. But they had plenty of spirit and they looked lightning fast. "They've got the speed," Chip muttered.

A few minutes later the game buzzer sounded and the teams lined up for the center tap. Then all the lights except those illuminating the court were dimmed and Chip was gripped by that empty, hollow-chest, straw-leg feeling which overwhelms most athletes just before the opening play of a game.

Coach Corrigan started the same team which had defeated mighty Southwestern in the finals of the Holiday Invitational Tournament. Sky Bollinger got the tap and immediately Tech showed its hand, each player moving rapidly out on the defense to meet his assigned opponent, sticking to him like glue, pressing and forcing him constantly back.

Soapy elbowed Chip in the ribs. "This is the first time I ever saw you in the stands. Now you'll learn how a fan feels about the game."

Chip found out about that quick enough. He found himself fighting and straining for every rebound and loose ball, and suffering and yelling when Tech scored. There wasn't much basketball being played down on the court. The game had developed into a wild, rushing, running, tumbling, up-and-

down-the-court melee, basketball in name only. After
five minutes of action, Tech led, 14 to 6.

"C'mon, c'mon," Soapy was yelling, shoving and
pushing and thumping Chip on the back. "Get the
ball! What's the matter with you guys? Look at that!"

Coach Corrigan had sent his team out on the floor
with instructions to use the same zone press which
had been so successful in the tournament. Surprisingly, the Tech coach had retaliated with the
same strategy. The Engineers were agile and fired
up and they pursued the ball as if they were tied
to it with an invisible string. They followed-in every
shot, double-teaming State's rebounders as soon as
they got the ball, advancing furiously in a wild
abandon which forced bad passes and resulted
in frequent interceptions. Neither team presented a
set pattern of attack or defense. There was no retreat and no let up.

Coach Corrigan finally managed to get a time-
out. The State players, sweat pouring off their faces,
circled him with their arms on each other's shoulders
and glanced uneasily at the scoreboard. Chip could
almost hear them saying: "What happened? What
happened?"

Corrigan was talking excitedly and Chip could
tell by his gestures that he was trying to get the
team to settle down. Then he tapped Butcher King
and Biz Gowdy and they ran to the scoring table
to report. Sky Bollinger and Bitsy Reardon pulled
their warm-up jackets over their shoulders and
slumped down on the bench. The buzzer shrilled
and the players of both teams promptly resumed
the mad, continuous scramble. No holds barred.

The officials were doing their best to keep up
with the fast pace but it was impossible. When a

foul was committed, the whistle was far behind the play. The boos of the fans who missed the infractions added to the tumult. At the half, Tech led by a score of 61 to 54. State's vaunted zone press had backfired.

The play of the second half was a duplication of the first. The fans shrieked, yelled, whistled, cheered, stamped their feet and pushed, jostled, elbowed, and swayed with each shot. The rival bands got into the act with loud blasts of horns and booming of drums, while the cheerleaders of both schools made vain efforts to initiate organized cheers.

"Jimmy will have to do it, Soapy," Chip said, glancing worriedly at the scoreboard.

"Somebody better do it," Soapy moaned.

Tech led by a score of 77 to 61 when Jimmy Lu Chung tried his individual control of the ball which had been so successful against Southwestern. But Burt Billings, Tech's wily coach, had assigned a small, speedy guard to play the clever dribbler. And this operator fell for none of the master dribbler's fakes, played Jimmy loose, and let him dribble all over the court until he tried for a score.

"It won't work," Chip breathed. "We've got to have points."

"Yeah," Soapy agreed. "We'd better go back to the press."

Chip nodded. "That's all that will keep us in the game."

State had abandoned the dribbling strategy now, and the press resulted in a lot of interceptions. But State couldn't quite catch up. Tech always managed to keep ahead. With two minutes to go, the Engineers led, 109 to 105. Then the game got completely out of hand.

A Tech player stabbed at the ball and knocked it out of Jimmy's hand and practically every player on the court dove for the recovery.

When the officials untangled the scrambling mob of players, Jimmy and his opponent got up swinging. It took the combined efforts of the officials and both coaches to separate the players. Coach Corrigan promptly removed Lu Chung, Butcher King, and Biz Gowdy and substituted Speed Morris, Rud Slater, and Dom Di Santis.

Both benches were on edge now and it showed in their angry, set faces. Out on the court, the players scrambled and dove for the ball. It was worse than fire-department basketball, more like football. The players took wild spills as a result of desperate attempts to gain or keep the ball, and all the time the big second hand on the game clock sped relentlessly around the clock.

Chip was yelling at the top of his voice but it was lost in the continuous crowd roar. "Come on, gang. Get the ball! You've got to score!"

But it was too late. The Tech players fought grimly to hold the lead, and the wild contest ended with players of both teams sprawled all over the court. The final score: Tech 111, State 107. The Engineers had upset the tournament champions.

Chip glanced gloomily at Soapy and slumped back down in his seat. Soapy followed suit and they sat there without a word while the fans filed down the steps. When the balcony emptied, they made their way slowly down the aisle to the mezzanine. The exit there was clogged up and the fans were packed close together, pushing and stumbling slowly along. Chip and Soapy sat down in two empty seats to wait for the crowd to clear.

Most of the Tech rooters had managed to beat the rush. But a few were caught behind with the slower-moving State fans. Chip and Soapy listened to the crowd's remarks.

"Corrigan lost the game," a State rooter said angrily. "Took Lu Chung, King, and Gowdy out just when we had a rally going."

"Right! The officials didn't put 'em out. Corrigan did!"

"You didn't see Burt Billings pulling any of *his* players out of the game."

"Aw, what are you cryin' about?" a hostile voice yelled. "Can't you take it?"

"We can take it, all right. And we'll take Tech the next time."

"And how!" a State supporter added. "Tech was lucky tonight. Half our team is crippled up."

"You mean Hilton?"

"That's right!"

"Wouldn't have made any difference tonight. Tech was red-hot!"

Chip was leaning on the back of the seat in front of him, looking down toward the press section. But he didn't see the writers who were busily typing away, recording the story of the upset. Chip was thinking about the game and how badly his teammates must be feeling at that moment. He squared his jaw and gripped his knee. Maybe he could play against Midwestern. . . .

Soapy jogged Chip's elbow. "There's Locke," he said, nodding toward the reporter who was busily typing away. "Looks like the cat that swallowed the canary. Wonder what's going on in that poisonous mind of his? Bad news for someone, I'll bet!"

CHAPTER 3

PLANS AND DREAMS

SOAPY glanced at his sleeping roommate and slipped quietly out of bed. He dressed hurriedly and headed for the corner newsstand. When he returned, Chip was dressing.

"What did I tell you last night!" Soapy said excitedly, waving a copy of the *News* in the air. "What did I tell you about Locke?"

"Bad?"

"And how! Listen to this headline. Quote: 'Tech surprises State. State athletic brass responsible for Tech upset.'

"How's that for a starter? Now get this: 'State's tournament champions were upset last night because of an antiquated schedule-making policy which is designed to insure State teams of easy victories against nonconference schools—' "

Chip stopped tying his necktie. "Nonconference schools!" he cried. "Why, most of them are tougher than the league teams!"

"That's what it says. Listen! 'The defeat may teach the State schedule architects a lesson. To wit: Big schools should play in their own class and forgo the

21

development of synthetic victory records at the expense of small-school setups.' "

"Some setup," Chip said. "They nearly ran us out of the gym."

Soapy nodded and continued reading. " 'Tech caught the Statesmen asleep, overconfident, and unprepared, and scored an unexpected 111 to 107 win. It was the Engineers' eighth consecutive victory of the season. With the exception of last night's win, Tech has met only second-class competition.' "

Soapy paused and eyed Chip expectantly. "What do you think of that?"

"It isn't very kind to Tech."

"*Kind?* Locke doesn't know the word."

"Doesn't he say anything about the game?"

"Plenty! Says there was a big fight near the end and that three State players were ejected."

"But that's not true. Coach took them out himself. They weren't ejected at all."

"Of course they weren't! The torch of truth means about as much to Locke as a secondhand toothpick. And that reminds me that I'm hungry. And we're going to be late if we don't step on it."

Chip had to force his pace to make the first class. There had been a lot of days during his freshman year and this year, too, when he had felt like skipping a class; days when the bruising knocks of a tough scrimmage or a tough game had left protesting muscles and aching bones.

But Chip had come to State with two great ambitions and he wasn't going to let a little physical discomfort interfere. First, he was determined to get a good education. Second, he was resolved to take advantage of all the expert coaching State's athletic staff provided. And from his very first day at

State, Chip had permitted nothing short of absolute sickness to sidetrack his plans and dreams.

Chip's path to a college education was not an easy one. His mother wanted to help, but all of Mary Hilton's earnings as a Valley Falls telephone supervisor were needed to maintain the family home. Chip was on his own, and proud of it. Fortunately, his experience during high-school days in the hometown drugstore had qualified him for the stockroom job at State Drug. So far, he was doing all right.

State's students were far from being in mourning following the Tech defeat. But they were hurt. Bad! It was a shock. A drop from the heights of elation to the dregs of disappointment in one fell swoop. But the unexpected loss failed to dampen their support of the team. They greeted the players warmly and Chip was thrilled by their loyalty.

"Tough loss, Hilton. Too bad you couldn't play."

"Yeah. Things would have been different."

"Hey, fella, get well quick! We need you!"

The loyalty of his classmates filled Chip with the determination to prove his appreciation. "I'll make up for it," he vowed. "One way or another . . ."

Lunch brought Chip and his Valley Falls pals together every day unless a class interfered. They had "adopted" a good-sized table in a corner of the cafeteria in Student Union. Today they were all on hand. Soapy, Speed, Biggie Cohen, and Red Schwartz were waiting when Chip arrived. At an adjoining table, Fireball Finley, Whitty Whittemore, and Jimmy Lu Chung were discussing the game.

"Hiya, Chip," Jimmy said glumly. "Not so good, eh?"

"You can't win them all, Jimmy."

"I don't mean that—I mean the fight. If you could call it a fight. I guess I haven't learned much about sportsmanship."

"Nonsense."

"It's not nonsense," Jimmy said earnestly. "I'll never know why I lost my head last night. And right in front of everybody in school. I'm a jerk."

"You weren't the only one," Fireball said. "How about King and Gowdy?"

"They haven't got the slightest thing to do with me. I lost the game."

"Get out!" Speed barked. "Basketball's a team game. *We* lost it."

"Guess you fellows read Locke's column this morning," Fireball said, making an obvious attempt to change the subject.

"Some difference between Locke and Bill Bell," Soapy said, pulling a copy of the *Herald* out of his pocket. "Bell says we were overconfident. Gives Corrigan a good plug for sportsmanship, too."

"I haven't seen Bill Bell's column," Speed said significantly, "but I'll bet *he* didn't call Tech a small-school setup."

"Right," Soapy agreed. "Bell says the athletic program at Tech is outstanding. No undue emphasis is placed on representative teams, but the school recognizes the value of competitive sports—"

"Hear! Hear!" Speed interrupted. "You memorize that?"

"And," Soapy continued glibly, "he says it's too bad Tech's present basketball club isn't playing a big-time schedule because it's a big-time team. Further, gentlemen, Mr. Bell says the local rivalry is good and should be exploited to the fullest extent."

"I always wondered who did Bell's ghost writing," Whitty said pointedly.

Soapy cleared his throat. "Ahem—er—thanks, Whitty." He rose to his feet. "Well, gentlemen, ahem . . . I regret that Mr. Hilton and I have been assigned an extremely exhaustive and demanding schedule by the State Board of Education. And, much as it grieves us, we must leave." He turned to Chip. "Shall we drop in on Professor Guidings and initiate our survey?"

"We certainly should," Chip said, grinning. "He's expecting us."

Chip's biology period lasted until four o'clock and practice was well under way when he reached the gym. He found Murph Kelly alone in the locker room and the trainer went right to work on his knee.

"Coach says you're not to go on the trip, Hilton. Says you are to rest until we get back."

"You sure? I feel fine."

"Of course I'm sure. Coach's orders. Oh, yes. Coach wants you to appear on Bill Bell's program. Bell's gonna pick you up here at five o'clock."

"Oh, no!"

"Don't blame me. Coach's orders."

Chip moaned disgustedly. "Why me, Murph?"

"Because Bill Bell wants you. That's why."

"But it's not fair to the other fellows."

"Stop being temperamental. Sports writers are important people, and sports need publicity. All kinds."

Kelly was still lecturing when Bill Bell knocked on the door. He entered and stood framed in the open door. "Hiya, Murph. Hello, Hilton. Guess we timed it about right."

As Bell drove Chip to the *Herald* building, he

quizzed him about his knee and then switched to the marksmanship tournament. "I sure hope your knee comes along, Chip. You're pretty important to the marksmanship tournament. We're going to have the biggest entry in the history of the event. Now about the program this afternoon . . ."

The *Herald* television studio was on the air when the sports editor and Chip tiptoed across the big room. Bell sat down behind a desk and motioned Chip to a chair beside him. While waiting, he leafed through several sports announcements. A minute or so later two cameramen maneuvered their cameras in front of the desk and a director followed, motioning for silence. Bill Bell smiled at Chip and faced the lens. Then a red spot glowed on the close-up camera and the director nodded his head.

"Good evening, sports fans, this is Bill Bell with the sports headlines of the day. Sports news was made today by Hal Deevers, national heavyweight champion of the world—Southwestern's almost invincible basketball machine—and the New York Knickerbockers . . . More about these items after a brief message from our sponsor."

Following the commercial, Bell followed through on the sports news. When he finished, he winked at Chip. "And now, I want to present a special guest. Fans, meet State's William "Chip" Hilton—"

The red eye of the camera panned over on Chip as Bell introduced him.

"This young man has made sports history in the year and a half he has been a student at State. He starred in three sports as a freshman and won the A.A.U. basketball marksmanship title. This past fall he piloted Red Ralston's varsity football team so brilliantly that he won All-America quarterback honors. Then, switching to basketball, he sparked State's hoop team to the Holiday Invitational Tournament championship and won the Most Valuable Player award."

Bell then questioned Chip about his knee and the extent of the injury and followed this by a switch to the Tech game. "This is a difficult question, Chip —probably painful, too—but what was *your* reaction to the big upset of your teammates last night? Was it a letdown after the big victory at Clinton?"

"I don't believe so, Mr. Bell."

"You don't think they underestimated Tech?"

Chip smiled. "If they did, it was only for about two minutes."

"There's no question about that. Now, what's your opinion of the Tech players?"

"All the Tech players are fine shooters, Mr. Bell, and they can really move."

"Should the team have national ranking?"

"Yes, indeed. It's one of the best teams I have seen this year."

"How do you think they would have made out in the tournament? Could they have given, say, Southwestern a good game?"

"I think so, sir. Playing as they did last night, they would have beaten any team."

"One last question. Do you think small schools, small colleges like Tech, should have the opportunity to compete for the national championship? Or should national recognition be restricted to large colleges and universities in terms of numerical equality?"

"I think all colleges, large or small, should have the opportunity to compete for the national championship. Naturally, observance of the N.C.A.A. eligibility rules are necessary. But the size of the student body has little bearing on the quality of its team. Basketball isn't like football. Seven or eight good basketball players are all that a championship team needs. I think Tech is a good example. The college is small but the team is great."

"I'm glad to hear you say that, Hilton. It also takes real sportsmanship to praise a rival after a bitter defeat.

"Well, I see that our time is about up and I want to thank you, Chip Hilton, for taking the time to come up here to meet our televiewers. I know that they join me in wishing you a quick recovery and an early return to the State basketball team. I don't have to add that the *Herald* and the marksmanship selection committee members are anxious to see if you will be the first champion to win the title two years in succession.

"That wraps it up for tonight, fans. So, until tomorrow evening, this is Bill Bell saying good night."

Thousands of loyal fans heard Bill Bell's telecast that evening. But down in Valley Falls, Chip's home town, Bell had a perfect score, a thousand-percent audience. Doc Jones, his pal John Schroeder, Mary Hilton, Petey Jackson, and hundreds of Chip's friends tuned in and were happy for him.

Jim Locke was also tuned in on the program. He liked to pick up material direct from his bitter rival's sports telecast.

When Bell finished, Locke grinned sardonically and snapped off his set. "This gets more interesting all the time," he observed aloud, moving toward his typewriter.

CHAPTER 4

A FINE SPORTSMAN

SOAPY was belligerently angry after reading Locke's column the next morning. "There oughta be a law, Chip," he said darkly.

"Why?"

"To take care of guys like this armchair sports expert. Listen—"

"I can't, Soapy. I'm late." Chip hurried away, trying to keep from limping and anxious to escape Soapy's tirade. But when he joined his pals in the Student Union for lunch, there was no escape.

"What are you going to do about it?" Soapy demanded.

"About what?" Chip parried.

"About Locke. He panned Bill Bell and you in his column this morning. Said you were Bell's yes man."

"So what?"

"You going to take that?"

"Sure. What else can I do?"

"You can punch him in the nose," Soapy said hotly.

"Sure," Chip agreed calmly, "and get thrown out

of school. Then he *would* have the right to spout off in his column. Nothing doing."

"Why, he inferred you were on Bell's marksmanship tourney payroll, too," Whitty said soberly. "That could get you into trouble."

"Not when it isn't true," Chip said softly. "Everyone knows that the A.A.U. runs the tournament and that every cent of expense is accounted for and published in the papers. No one would believe Locke on that score."

"Why pick on you?" Fireball mused.

"Perhaps it's because I agree with Mr. Bell that Tech is a top-flight team."

"That's it," Jimmy said quickly. "Locke isn't riding Chip. He's feuding with Bill Bell. He rides anyone who is on Bell's side. He's been fighting with Bell for years. Or trying to . . ."

"I didn't want to go on that program," Chip said ruefully, "but Murph said it was Coach's orders. No more for me."

"Let's forget it," Fireball interposed. "My coach used to say he was happy when he got his name on the sports pages, whether he was getting panned or praised. You going with the team this afternoon, Chip?"

"No. I would just take up space. Anyway, Murph has enough to do on a road trip without taking care of me. Two games in two days is tough. Well, I've got to go to class. Good luck, Speed, Jimmy. You can take 'em!"

But Speed, Jimmy, and their teammates couldn't "take 'em." Midwestern defeated State by a score of 84 to 80. Chip and Soapy got the news at Pete's Place after work and didn't even wait for a sandwich.

Saturday was cold and rainy, and business at State Drug was slow all morning. Late that afternoon, when Soapy reported the Western score, gloom settled on the store like a black London fog. The Statesmen lost their third game in a row that afternoon at Western, 91 to 90.

Chip was so despondent that he again passed up the after-work gathering at Pete's Place. And it was raining so steadily that he was glad to let Soapy drive him home in Mitzi Savrill's car. It was pouring when they stopped at a service station for gasoline; the rain was beating down on the windshield and windows so heavily that Chip could scarcely see the face of the attendant who reluctantly approached the car.

"You *would* come now," the man growled, shielding his eyeglasses with his hand and peering at Soapy through the open window. "How many?"

"Sorry, old-timer," Soapy said sympathetically, extending a dollar bill. "The union of fog participles, ahem——"

"Particles," Chip corrected.

"As I was saying," Soapy continued, "the union of fog particles and the restraint of their progress toward the earth is in the power of no man— Give me an even dollar's worth, please. Gasoline, of course."

The man pursed his lips and glared angrily at Soapy. "Yah!" he snarled disgustedly. "Another smart college kid. Huh! A dollar's worth! And in all this rain!"

"You shouldn't kid an old man like that, Soapy," Chip said reprovingly.

Soapy nodded. "You're right. Especially in weather like this. I'm a dope."

It was a bad night to drive and Chip was relieved when they reached Jeff and he could go to bed. But he couldn't get to sleep. And when Soapy returned they talked a long time in the dark about the quick disaster which had overtaken the team.

Sunday dawned clear and cold. Chip awoke at daylight and glanced out the open window. Then he sighed contentedly and pulled the blankets up under his chin. This is the life, he was thinking. Now for a good, long snooze. No school and no need to get up until time to go to church. It seemed only a second later when Soapy shook him awake. "Hey, Chip! Wake up!"

Chip looked at the redhead in amazement. "What's wrong with you?" he demanded. "This is my morning to sleep late, remember?"

"I know, I know, Chip," Soapy apologized. "It's the train—"

"Train? What train?"

"The nine thirty. The train the team is coming in on . . ."

"What about it?"

"Well, the team lost and—"

Chip checked him. "Good idea! I'll be dressed in a second."

"But your knee."

"Don't worry. I'll be all right."

Soapy shook his head worriedly. "I didn't expect you to go, Chip. I just needed a little help."

"What kind of help?"

"Well, you're president of Jeff. Right? So, if you say the word, everybody goes! Right?"

"Right! Pass the word."

Soapy passed the word. And how! The clang-clang-clang of the fire alarm brought every student

in Jeff flooding out in the corridors on every floor.
"Where's the fire?"

"Somebody call the fire department!"

"I've got an extinguisher. Now what do I do?"

"Put out the fire, dope."

"Yeah, sure! But where is it?"

"Nobody knows."

"Oh, oh! What are you laughing about, Smith?"

Soapy took off. "Pass the word!" he shouted.
"Chip's orders! Everybody meets the basketball team
at the station at nine thirty. See you there!"

Soapy was waiting in a taxi when Chip reached
the street. And just as the cab moved away from
the curb, Jeff's residents came streaming down the
walk, falling enthusiastically in line to show their
support of the team.

Thirty minutes later State's varsity hoop squad
detrained and stared unbelievingly at the crowded
platform. But only for a second. Soapy leaped on a
baggage truck and led the cheers.

"Yea, team! Yea, State! Who do we appreciate?"

"Corrigan!" Chip yelled.

"Corrigan!" the gang repeated. "Corrigan!"

"Say it again!" Soapy yelled.

"Corrigan!"

And so it went. Right down the line from Coach
Jim Corrigan to his assistant, Henry Rockwell, to
Captain Kirk Markley and Captain Randy Thornhill
and Butcher King, Jimmy Lu Chung, Speed Morris
and all the others with a last big cheer for Murph
Kelly.

Then the rally broke up, the players piling into
waiting taxis, their weariness and dejection blasted
away by Jeff's loyal ovation. Soapy ushered Speed,
Jimmy, and Chip to his cab and they took off.

Jim Corrigan and Henry Rockwell remained on the platform watching the taxis stream away. Corrigan sighed deeply. "Kids are great, Rock. Makes me feel wonderful when I see a bunch of kids do something so spontaneous and real as this little rally."

"I've been feeling that way for thirty-nine years, Jim."

"Maybe coaching isn't so tough after all," Corrigan said softly.

The young coach and the veteran stood quietly on the platform, impervious to the cold, each steeped in thought. Corrigan broke the silence. "Say, Rock, we ought to do something for Smith. I've never felt he had a fair chance to make the squad."

"You had to cut someone, Jim. Soapy didn't have time to get adjusted after football, that's all. Chip and Speed are natural athletes. All sports come easy for them. Soapy has to pay a price for everything he does."

Corrigan nodded. "I guess you're right, but it seems a shame. I never knew an athlete with more enthusiasm."

"Or more loyalty," Rockwell added. "Well, let's go home."

Meanwhile, the taxi bearing Chip, Soapy, Speed, and Jimmy was speeding toward Jeff, the conversation of the occupants centered around the twin road defeats.

"What happened?" Soapy asked.

"They were too good for us, that's all," Speed said ruefully.

Jimmy nodded agreement. "Right! We fought, all right. Both games. But we've got to face it. Without Chip we haven't got a scoring punch."

"That's silly," Chip interrupted. "You beat the

greatest team in the country with me on the bench."

"Sure," Jimmy agreed. "But we surprised them with our zone press. Now, everybody's ready for it."

"Tech set the pattern, Chip," Speed said. "Coach Billings scouted us at Clinton and saw the difference between our press and the usual kind and he got Tech ready for it. Now, the other teams are ready. And without you to give us thirty or forty points a game we haven't got a chance. Especially against the *good* teams."

"Of all the nonsense—" Chip began.

"Nonsense nothing," Soapy cut in, "it's true. No team can afford to lose a thirty-point player."

"He's so right, Chip," Speed said earnestly. "I sure hope you can play Wednesday night. If we lose to Cathedral, we might as well turn in our uniforms. They haven't won a game all year."

"Think you can play, Chip?" Jimmy asked.

Chip nodded. "I'll play."

Chip's decision to get back into action was strengthened further that afternoon. On his way home from church, he met a number of townspeople and students. Many inquired about his knee. All were interested in finding out when he would be back in the line-up. When he reached Jeff, he found the *News* and the *Herald* opened to the sports pages.

Halfway down Jim Locke's column in the *News*, Soapy had underlined a phrase: "What *is* wrong with Chip Hilton? Is the brilliant scoring star resting on his tournament laurels?"

That hit home but Chip felt a little better after reading the *Herald*. Soapy had underlined a couple of phrases in Bill Bell's column, too. Chip breathed a little easier as he read the first one. "The Statesmen's third loss in a row serves to reiterate my previous statement that Chip Hilton is irreplaceable and of vital importance to Jim Corrigan's team."

"I wish he'd stop writing that stuff," Chip murmured. Then he read the other paragraph Soapy had marked. "This writer talked to Coach Jim Corrigan early this morning about his star scorer and I should like to quote his reply: 'We need Chip Hilton badly, but no basketball victory, nor basketball season, is important enough to warrant the use of an athlete as long as there is any chance of hampering his improvement from an injury.' End quote. . . .

"That reply, fans, marks Coach Jim Corrigan as a fine sportsman."

"You can say that again," Chip said aloud.

Chip took a long walk that afternoon to limber up his knee and spent the rest of the day "hitting the books."

All day Monday—at Student Union, in his classes, and on the campus—Chip's classmates and friends asked about his knee. But behind their interest, Chip could sense the wish for his return to the team. "You're walking O.K., Hilton. Couldn't you give it a try?"

"What does Doc Terring say?"

"Gosh, I thought for sure we would win the conference this year."

Chip reported for practice that afternoon determined to play. But he ran into trouble. Murph Kelly was sympathetic but obdurate. "Work out? Nothing doing! Not until Doc gives me an O.K. The heck with what people say! Legs is prima donnas. Just like athletes!"

"Can I see Dr. Terring today?"

"Nope," Kelly said shortly. "Maybe Wednesday. Not before."

Chip's jaw firmed and for a second an angry retort formed in his mind. But he said nothing. Murph Kelly was his friend and you couldn't be angry with someone who was trying to help you. "All right, Murph," he said, trying to conceal his anger. "I'll wait."

Tuesday was a rough day. The pressure was on from every side. The only encouraging event was the arrival of the new brace Dr. Terring had ordered. It fitted his knee like a glove. "Oh, boy!" Chip exulted. "I can do it. I can play."

The action at State Drug tapered off around eight thirty and Chip put through a call to his mother in Valley Falls. When he got through, Chip explained that the brace had arrived and that his knee felt fine. "It's a perfect fit, Mother," he explained.

"The knee is the thing, Chip," Mrs. Hilton remonstrated.

"But I've got to play, Mother. I'm on a spot."

"When are you going to see Dr. Terring again?"

"Tomorrow afternoon."

"Well, Chip, if he says you can play . . . all right. But if it means a lot of pain . . ."

"If Doc Terring gives me permission to play against Cathedral, Mother, I'll be able to stand the pain!"

CHAPTER 5

THE VICTORY TRAIN

Dr. Mike Terring, an avid sports enthusiast, liked his job as State's chief medical officer. But the task which confronted him this particular afternoon was extremely distasteful. Terring was keenly aware of Chip's importance to State's basketball team and he also realized the emotional factors involved. But Dr. Terring was, first of all and always first, a physician. He shrugged his broad shoulders and turned to Murph Kelly. "What do you think, Murph?"

"He's moving pretty good, Doc," Kelly said. "And the new brace—"

"Oh, yes," Terring interrupted. "I wanted to ask you about it."

"It's fine, Doc. I'm sure I can play."

Dr. Terring hesitated. "Well," he said reluctantly, "if Murph puts a good bandage under the brace I don't see how you can do much damage. . . ." He eyed the trainer questioningly.

Kelly nodded and turned away, muttering something unintelligible. Chip followed jubilantly and started for home, anxious to tell his pals the good news. But when he reached the door he stopped in dismay. A storm was blowing and wild gusts of wind sprayed cold sleet in every direction.

It took him half an hour to cover a distance which usually required less than ten minutes. When he reached Jeff, his leg was cold and tired. Speed was studying in the library on the first floor and saw Chip come in. He rushed out into the hall. "Where have you been? You crazy?"

Chip explained the result of his visit to Dr. Terring. As soon as Speed heard the good news, he headed for the telephone. "You get some rest," he called over his shoulder. "I'm going to call Soapy."

It was six thirty when Soapy appeared with sandwiches and milk. The redhead was excited and happy. "Boy, oh, boy! Things will be different now! Wish I could see it. Look! Mitzi told me to drive you fellows to the game and then hurry back to work. But she said I was to come back for you at ten thirty."

Soapy drove them to Alumni Gym, and by that time the sleet had changed to a wet snow. "That's a help," Soapy said gratefully. "Looked as if we were in for a real ice storm. See you at ten thirty."

Murph Kelly had alerted Chip's teammates and they let him have it as soon as he opened the door.

"Atta boy, Chip!"

"We'll get 'em now!"

"This is the best news since the tournament!"

Coach Corrigan and Henry Rockwell came in while Kelly was bandaging his knee and they examined the brace carefully. "Loosen up slow, Chip," Coach Corrigan said. "I may not use you, but I want to be sure you're right just in case . . ." He turned to the blackboard and sketched several diagrams. "All right, fellows, give me your attention."

It was a disagreeable night, but surprisingly there was a good turnout for the game. When State ran out on the floor the loyal fans gave the team a rousing reception. Then they realized Chip was back in uniform, and the applause increased. The fans watched every move he made, hoping that he was back in shape. But the brace restricted free use of his knee, and it was easy to see that his movements were hampered.

Chip's shooting eye was still on the beam, and his shots began dropping through the hoop from all angles. Then the referee's whistle cut through the noise of the crowd and the game was on.

State led from the opening toss and the score at the half was: State 39, Cathedral 34. Corrigan made no move to use Chip during this period because the Statesmen seemed to have the game well under control. But in the second half, Cathedral scored three quick baskets and took the lead, 40 to 39.

Markley called "time" and the fans began to chant: "We want Hilton! We want Hilton!"

Corrigan glanced at Chip uncertainly, but Murph Kelly murmured something in the coach's ear and the same team went back in the game. Cathedral kept right on going, and with the score 47 to 43 in favor of the visitors, Corrigan called for a time-out. There were thirteen minutes left to play, now, and the fans began chanting in unison over and over:

"We want Hilton! We want Hilton!"

Corrigan shook his head grimly and turned to the bench. "All right, Chip. Give it a whirl. But let me know if it's no go."

"I'll be all right, Coach," Chip said, adding a fervent, "I hope," under his breath.

When Chip joined the team on the floor his team-

mates were Randy Thornhill, Sky Bollinger, Speed
Morris, and Jimmy Lu Chung. Chip breathed a
sigh of relief. Speed and Jimmy could do the cutting
and he could handle the ball and set up the plays.
But it didn't work out that way.

Speed Morris had played with Chip for three
years, knew how to work his pal's favorite shooting
screens, fast-moving clear-outs, and the give-and-go
plays which gave Chip room for his set shots. And it
worked. Speed set up four straight shots and Chip
hit for three. During this time, Cathedral scored but
once and Chip's third tally tied the score.

Then Jimmy Lu Chung got the idea, and he too
began to set Chip up for the long set shots. The
crowd was in an uproar as State and Cathedral
matched baskets right down the stretch. Chip felt
little pain, but the brace hampered his starts and
stops, and it was impossible for him to muster enough
speed for a drive. So he concentrated on the long
sets. With a minute to play, the score was 81 to 81
and State had the ball. Randy Thornhill got Corrigan's sign for a time-out then, and the team circled
their coach in front of the State bench.

"Let Jimmy hold it for one shot," Coach Corrigan
said decisively. "You take it out of bounds, Chip,
and pass to Jimmy. Speed, you set the pick. The
rest of you cut toward the basket but don't charge
anyone. Got it? O.K. Let's go!"

Chip took the ball out of bounds at the middle
of the court. When time was in, Speed set a block
for Jimmy in the outer half of the free-throw circle,
and Chip hit the little dribbler with a perfect pass
at the head of the circle.

Jimmy dribbled slowly to the right and glanced
at the clock. Then he began his dribble freeze. Chip

and Speed opened up the backcourt, and Sky Bollinger and Randy Thornhill went to the base-line corners. Jimmy froze the ball all by himself, dribbling with such uncanny skill that it looked as easy as controlling a yo-yo. As the little spark plug played out the clock and kept control of the ball for the last shot, the applause of the home fans grew and grew in wild acclaim.

Then the game clock's second hand ticked into the red-tinted final fifteen seconds of the game and Jimmy began to maneuver for position. His opponent now knew what to expect and kept as far away as possible without giving Jimmy too much room for a quick set. But he underestimated Jimmy's feinting ability. Jimmy faked right, left, and then sped to the right, gaining a half-step lead on his guard. At the free-throw line he leaped high in the air and thrust the ball over his head for a jump shot.

Then Sky Bollinger's tall opponent made a mistake; he thought it was the real McCoy and switched to stop the shot. Jimmy faked the shot with his empty right hand and zipped the ball to Sky with a cross-arm bounce pass. Bollinger was all alone when he dunked the ball through the hoop to win the game, 83 to 81.

Chip's leg ached but he was happy. After his shower, he waited until the trainer finished with the other players. Then Kelly gave his knee a short whirlpool treatment and bandaged it tightly. "You can loosen the bandage when you go to bed," he said when Chip protested. "Personally, I think you were a fool to play tonight. If I had my way, you would turn in your uniform right now."

Kelly turned abruptly away, but as Chip and Speed were leaving, he growled, "Good night."

When Chip and Speed reached the street, the storm was in full blast. Through the darkness they saw Mitzi's car with Soapy at the wheel. They hurried toward the car and Soapy opened the back door before they reached the curb. "Nice going, guys," Soapy cried. "Now we're back on the victory train." He reached back and patted Chip's knee. "Hear you got sixteen points, Chipper. Great! Your leg O.K.?"

"Never mind my leg. You be careful with this car. It's a bad night."

Soapy dropped his two buddies off at Jeff and started back to State Drug. Just as he turned off the campus he noticed that the gas needle was quivering over the red danger signal. "Oh, no," he muttered to himself. "Not again! And me with only fifty cents. Doesn't Mitzi ever put any gas in this thing?"

Just ahead, the lights of the Triangle Service Station streamed across the street and Soapy drove to the last pump. He turned off the motor and was out of the car before the engine stopped, frantically searching through his pockets. "Fifty cents!" he moaned, ducking his head as the attendant approached.

"What's that?" the old man asked sharply.

"Fifty cents' worth," Soapy said in a muffled voice as he climbed back in the car.

"Fifty cents! You mean a half dollar's worth of gasoline? I'll bet you're one of those smart college students. Huh! Fifty cents . . ."

The man put the gas in the tank and snapped the lid down abruptly on the fender. Yanking his hat down over his face, he took the proffered half dollar and stalked back through the wet snow.

Soapy drove slowly and carefully down Main Street. A block from State Drug he recognized Jane Adams, another of George Grayson's employees, standing all alone on the corner. Soapy pulled to the curb and opened the car door. "Hey!" he called. "Jane! It's me! Soapy. Get in. I'll drive you home."

Jane peered in at Soapy and then ducked into the car. "What a night!" she gasped, shivering. "I'm nearly frozen. I've been standing on that corner since ten thirty. Mother will be worried sick."

"What time is it now?"

"Five minutes after eleven," Jane said disgustedly, pointing to the dash clock. She verified it with her wrist watch, holding her arm up to the window. "Exactly right. It would be, knowing Mitzi. Someone ought to do something about the bus service in this town."

The car passed State Drug at that moment and Soapy cast an agonized glance through the window. The store was practically empty. "Oh, oh," he whispered frantically. "I'm in trouble. I'll never make it."

"What did you say?" Jane asked.

"Where do you live? How far is it?"

"About twenty minutes by car. A little longer, perhaps, on a night like this."

The car leaped forward as Soapy lunged down on the accelerator, the wheels spinning and screeching before they got traction.

"Be careful!" Jane gasped. "You're driving Mitzi's car, remember."

"You're telling me," Soapy groaned, glancing at the gas gauge.

It was exactly twenty-five minutes after eleven when Soapy pulled up in front of Jane's house. "My, you drive fast," Jane said. "Exactly twenty minutes. Good night, Soapy, and thanks a million."

Soapy waited impatiently till Jane had entered the house before he started back. Fortunately, there was little traffic and he made good time. A few minutes later he felt the car sway and he slowed down. Then the back of the car suddenly swerved and slid nearly off the road. Soapy braked down and got out to take a look.

The front and back tires on his side were all right. But the right rear end of the car slanted down and Soapy's heart sank. "Oh, no," he moaned, moving around the back of the car. One glance was enough; his premonition was confirmed. The tire was as flat as a pancake.

"Now you're in the soup," Soapy told himself, opening the trunk and lifting the spare out in the road. "Now where's the jack . . ."

He searched every inch of the dark trunk but there was no jack. "No jack!" he cried. "Impossible! There *has* to be a jack."

He searched the back seat and then the front and under the cushions. But there was no jack anywhere. Not even a lug wrench.

"Good thing it happened to me," Soapy muttered. "What if it had been Mitzi? Gosh, she wouldn't even know where to start."

The thought was small consolation. Soapy remembered that Mitzi lived near the campus and would have had help in five minutes. He dimmed the lights and stood out in the middle of the road in the wet snow. Several cars slowed down until they got past him and then sped away.

Soapy walked back to the car and looked at the clock. "Eleven forty-five," he groaned. "I'll have to walk back to town or get to a telephone. I'm ruined. Mitzi will never speak to me again."

Then he saw a car slowing down, the lights picking their way through the snow. The car gradually came to a stop. "Having trouble, buddy?" a cheery voice called.

Soapy was almost in tears. "I sure am! I've got a flat and I don't have a jack or a lug wrench. Or any sense!" he concluded.

"Got a spare?"

"That's all."

"That's enough. Don't worry. We'll have you on your way in a jiffy. Come on, gang. Give me a hand."

The speaker, followed by two companions, piled out of the car. They produced a jack and a lug wrench from their own car and went to work. Laughing, talking, and joking, the three fellows worked together as efficiently as a racing-car pit crew.

"There you are," the tall fellow said, straightening up and wiping his hands on a handkerchief. "Take it easy now."

Before Soapy could do more than mumble "thanks" they were back in their car and gone. The redhead drove more carefully now, and it was twelve fifteen when he reached Main and Tenth. State Drug was blacked out, but the lights from Pete's Place were blazing out through the snow.

"An hour late," Soapy groaned.

He parked in front of the restaurant and peered through the window. Right in the line of his vision, sitting at a table facing the door, was the love of Soapy's life.

Soapy stood out in the middle of the road

CHAPTER 6

THE NIGHT RIDER

MITZI SAVRILL, Fireball, Whitty, and Jimmy Lu Chung were sitting at the table. Pete stood behind the counter. He saw Soapy first. "Well, look who's here," he said. "The night rider!"

"I'll bet he had engine trouble," Fireball said.

"Uh, uh," Whitty corrected. "He had a flat tire."

Mitzi got slowly to her feet. "He could have run out of gas," she said lightly. "There wasn't much in the tank."

"Blonde or brunette, Soapy?" Fireball asked.

Soapy's face turned fiery red. "Aw, you know me better than that, Fireball." He turned to Mitzi. "Honest, Mitzi, I had a flat. And there wasn't a jack in the car and— Well, I'm sorry I'm late. I guess your folks will be upset, but—"

Mitzi flashed him one of her heartbreaking smiles and Soapy nearly collapsed. "It's all right, Soapy," she said. "I called home. There's no harm done. Come on. I'll give you all a lift."

Chip was still awake when he heard the car stop in front of Jeff. He snapped on his bed lamp and waited until Soapy opened the door. The sight which

48

met his eyes gave him a shock. "What happened to you?" he asked, staring at his snow-soaked pal.

"Oh, boy!" Soapy moaned. "Did *I* ever have trouble! What a night."

"What happened? Where were you?"

Soapy briefed Chip on his night's adventure, skipping over certain nonessentials but telling enough about his experience to arouse his pal's sympathy.

"Better take a hot shower and put another blanket on your bed," Chip said. "Now forget all about it and get a good night's rest."

Chip's leg was stiff and sore the next morning, but by the end of his last morning class it had loosened up. He walked briskly across the campus to the Student Union and found Fireball and Whitty already seated at the corner table. They were waiting impatiently for Soapy. "Now what are you up to?" Chip asked.

"You'll see," Fireball said cryptically. "Did you see Soapy when he got home last night?"

Chip smiled. "I sure did."

"Hush!" Whitty cautioned. "Here he comes."

Soapy approached warily. Placing his loaded tray on the table, he edged self-consciously into a chair. "What are you guys so serious about?" he asked.

"We're broke," Whitty said. "How about lending us ten?"

"Me?" Soapy asked incredulously. "When did *I* ever have any money?"

"Thought you might be carrying a roll," Whitty said, spreading a copy of the *Herald* on the table. "Look at this," he said significantly, tapping the headline. "Right on the front page. Read it!"

At the top of the paper in bold print was the news item:

TRIANGLE GAS STATION ROBBED

Lone Holdup Bandit Makes Clean Getaway

The fourth in a series of holdups occurred at eleven forty-five last night at the Triangle Service Station. The lone stick-up artist obtained over a hundred dollars. George Welsh, age fifty-five, was the attendant in charge and described the suspect as being young, weighing around one hundred and eighty pounds, and about six feet in height.

Mr. Welsh gave police a good description of the man but was unable to furnish the license number of the car because of the heavy snow. The bandit was driving a dark, four-door car with a white top. Welsh was sure the man had purchased gasoline at the station less than an hour earlier. The police found one important clue.

"Well—" Soapy said, looking from Fireball to Whitty.

"Flat tire, eh?" Whitty commented suggestively.

"Black car with a white top," Fireball said thoughtfully. "Hmm."

Chip didn't like it. "Now wait a minute, fellows," he said lightly. "This isn't funny."

Fireball burst out laughing and pointed to Soapy's face. "We're just kidding."

Soapy grinned. "Sure," he said, "it was easy."

"What did you do with the money?" Fireball asked. "Put it in the flat tire?"

"The police will check *that*," Whitty said, nodding his head wisely.

"Maybe I ought to surrender," Soapy suggested.

"Don't worry," Fireball said. "The paper says the bandit made a *clean* getaway. Heck, we can give you a perfect alibi. You were as dirty as a coal miner just coming home from work."

Chip glanced at the clock and hastily gathered up his tray of dishes. "Don't you fellows have any fifth-period classes?" he interrupted. "I've got to hurry. See you tonight."

Dr. Terring showed up before practice that afternoon to check Chip's leg. "Pretty stiff, eh?" he asked, punching the ligament.

Chip nodded. "A little. But I think it's better."

"Appears about the same to me," Dr. Terring said. "Are you sure the wish isn't father to the thought?"

"No, sir. It isn't paining a bit this afternoon."

Dr. Terring shook his head. "Pain or no pain, the ligament is still swollen. Injuries take time."

"But you said it would be all right if I rested between games."

"I said it *might* be all right." Dr. Terring turned to the trainer. "Excuse him today, Murph. Let him shoot around a little tomorrow and you watch him."

Chip dressed quickly and caught the downtown bus. When he arrived at State Drug, Whitty and Fireball were still razzing Soapy.

"Flat tire, eh?"

"Now it says on the front page of the paper . . ."

"I still say it was a blonde."

Chip was caught in the cross fire and took it all in, noting Soapy's quick glance toward Jane Adams and the return wink. Jane was working her way through State and her hours were the same as his own. She quit work at ten thirty each night, while Mitzi seldom completed balancing the slips and cash register before eleven o'clock.

"That's the answer," Chip told himself. "Soapy took her home and had a flat tire and he doesn't want Mitzi to find it out."

Murph Kelly let Chip dress Friday afternoon. "Shoot around at the practice basket, Chip, but take it easy."

Coach Corrigan was working the varsity on the main court and toward the end of practice Murph Kelly wandered down to Chip. "How's it going?"

"Not too bad, Murph. If I didn't have to wear the brace, I guess I could move a lot better."

Kelly grinned. "Sure! Sure you could. But the purpose of the brace is to keep the ligament under control. The brace prevents stretching and sudden strains. By the way, Coach has a visitor." He hooked a thumb toward the bleachers.

Coach Corrigan was standing on the side line, talking to a tall, stoop-shouldered man dressed in sports clothes. "Locke," Kelly said disgustedly. "He's got a lot of nerve busting in here. Coach ought to throw him out."

"Sports need publicity," Chip said significantly, smiling at the angry trainer.

"Not the kind he writes. Oh, oh, here he comes. See you later."

Chip had met Jim Locke a number of times and had always felt uncomfortable in his presence. Now, he thought of the article in which the caustic writer had referred to him as Bill Bell's yes man, and he felt almost antagonistic. Locke's personal appearance was enough to cause an instant dislike by anyone, but Chip had tried to keep his feelings neutral. Now he appraised the man more critically.

The sports writer had a long, thin nose and affected a short mustache and sideburns. His clothes would have been more in keeping with a high-school sophomore. As he approached, Chip moved toward the free-throw line, trying to avoid conversation. But Locke followed him right out on the court.

"Hello, Hilton. What's this? A sort of individual practice?"

"I guess you could call it that, Mr. Locke," Chip said calmly. "Murph Kelly won't let me do much running."

"Is your leg really that bad?"

"Dr. Terring and Murph seem to think so."

"Well, anyway," Locke said slyly as he sauntered away, "it gives you a chance to practice your shots for Bell's shooting tourney."

Chip was seething inside, but he controlled the impulse to strike back at the sarcastic writer. With a man of Locke's type, it was wiser to ignore anything he said or wrote. Chip got a little consolation from the thought that most of the man's readers were familiar with his exaggerations.

At nine o'clock that evening Mary Hilton called Chip from Valley Falls. She was worried about his leg and wondered if he should be playing basketball. "Are you giving your knee plenty of rest?"

Chip reassured his mother and told her he was feeling fine. But he wasn't so sure. His leg was throbbing with pain, brace or no brace.

But Saturday morning, when the Statesmen took the bus for the Northern State game, Chip was aboard. His teammates were relieved when he showed up and they voiced their feelings.

"You're our good-luck charm, Chipper."

"He sure is! Whether he plays or not."

"I'll play," Chip said stoutly.

Kelly bandaged his knee unusually tight that night. Chip could scarcely move. But he got a break.

Northern State used a two-one-two zone and Chip had a picnic. Coach Corrigan set up a one-three-one attack and Chip scored fourteen goals from the field and four free throws for a total of thirty-two points.

But it was still a bitter struggle. Northern was aggressive and hustled all the way, and State couldn't get through the chasers for close shots. Chip's set shots were the decisive factor and State eked out a close victory, 77 to 75.

It was a long bus ride back and Murph Kelly made the driver stop at frequent intervals. Each time, when the other players went outside for a stretch of coffee and sandwiches, Kelly kept Chip in the bus and made him walk up and down the aisle.

"I'm moving more now than I did in the game," Chip protested.

"That's what you get for playing," Kelly growled.

The bus reached University at two o'clock in the morning and the driver drove directly to the dormitories and residences of the players. Soapy was asleep and Chip managed to get into bed without waking him up. It seemed as if only a few minutes had passed when he woke up and glanced at the clock. It was nine o'clock and Soapy's bed was made up. "He's gone for the papers," Chip murmured.

While Chip waited, half awake and half asleep, he thought about his pal's generous nature and his constant efforts to help his friends. A fellow usually had only a few tried-and-true friends during his whole life, but Chip was thinking that he was one of the luckiest fellows in the world. He had so many friends he could scarcely count them.

Soapy was number one, of course. After the redhead came Henry Rockwell, Mr. Grayson, Biggie Cohen, Speed Morris, Red Schwartz, Fats Ohlson,

Jimmy Lu Chung, Fireball Finley, Whitty Whittemore, and Pete Thorp. And back in Valley Falls there was Doc Jones, Mr. Schroeder, Petey Jackson and . . .

The next time Chip awakened, Soapy was sitting on his bed reading. Chip watched his pal through half-closed eyes. Soapy was muttering angrily and gritting his teeth.

Chip could restrain himself no longer. "What's so serious?"

Soapy leaped to his feet. "Hey!" he shouted, striking a fighting pose. "You scared me to death . . .

"Say! Some game. Nice going! We got the score at Pete's last night after work." Soapy jabbed the paper. "You see this? Jim Locke again."

Soapy shook the paper angrily and read aloud: " 'Has Chip Hilton been trying to prove State can't win without him? If so, he is so right!' " Soapy balled the paper in his hands and hurled it at the wastepaper basket. "How about that guy, Chip?"

Chip cracked his right fist into the palm of his left hand. "I wish . . ."

"Wish what?"

"Nothing, Soapy. You should know what to expect from Locke by this time. What does Bill Bell say?"

Soapy sat down on the bed and picked up the *Herald*. "That's better," he murmured as he read.

"What's better?"

"Bell. He says State deserves a lot of credit for its fight. And he says you could help the team even if you had to shoot from the bench. He gives the marksmanship tourney a good plug, too. And he says that Tech is one of the best teams in the country. They won again last night. That's ten in a row.

Oh, I gotta go. See you later. Gotta go on an errand for Mitzi."

"What kind of errand?"

Soapy hesitated. "It's kinda personal but— Well, I'm going to wash her car. Gotta pay her back for— Well, see you later."

"Wait a minute. I'll help you."

"Nothing doing! It's my responsibility. And, well . . ."

Chip grinned and nodded. "I understand, old pal. By the way, I want you to know, Soapy, that *I* know exactly why you borrowed Mitzi's car. And I know why you suddenly have an errand when it's necessary for me to do a little walking . . ."

Soapy's face fell and Chip continued hurriedly, "It's swell of you to do it, Soapy. I guess I don't have to tell you what it means to me. Anyway, I guess we understand each other. We always did."

Soapy took off and Chip got up and dressed slowly. He read the front page of the *Herald* and then started for church. After lunch, he hit the books. When Soapy returned a little later, the redhead joined him in study. After dinner, they took a short walk and then hit the books again.

On Monday morning Chip's knee felt as strong as ever. It seemed even stronger that afternoon when he reported to Murph Kelly. But he couldn't convince the trainer that he should practice. The sports veteran knew all about overconfident athletes.

"Take it easy," Kelly said. "You're not practicing. And tomorrow," he added, "you're going to do nothing but shoot a few baskets. Now beat it! And if you're going down to State Drug, take a taxi."

Chip laughed. "You don't care what I do with my money, do you?"

"I care what you do with your money, all right," Kelly growled, "but I want to protect that knee, too." He paused briefly and then continued gruffly, "Go on! Get out of here! I'm wasting my breath."

Eddie Redding arrived from school shortly after Chip reached State Drug and they worked steadily until Soapy joined them at six o'clock. The redhead rushed into the stockroom and began searching the pockets of his coat. "It's gone!" he said, looking disgustedly at Chip. "I can't find my laundry check. I must have lost it."

"Where is the place?"

"Two blocks up the street."

"Wait. I'll go with you."

The laundry service occupied little more space than one of the hallways which lined the street. A high counter faced the door and rows of shelves extended to the ceiling, all piled high with bundles. A young man was alone in the small room busily sorting clothing. "Good evening," he said, advancing to the counter. "Can I help you?"

"I hope!" Soapy said. "I haven't got a clean shirt to my name."

"Do you have your ticket?"

"That's the trouble," Soapy explained. "I lost it."

The young fellow smiled. "You know the old saying: No tickee, no shirtee."

Soapy nodded. "I know. But I lost it."

"That's all right. I think we can find it. Do you remember the number?"

"No, I don't."

"Tell him what you brought in," Chip suggested.

Soapy explained that there were eight shirts in the package. While he was talking, another customer entered and waited patiently. Soapy stepped aside and addressed the man. "Go ahead, mister. I've lost my ticket."

"I have plenty of time," the stranger said quietly.

Meanwhile, the clerk was checking through the bundles, studying the slips on each. He stopped suddenly and pulled a package from a top shelf. "Eight shirts," he said cryptically. He placed the bundle on the counter and studied the ticket on the front of the package. "Can you identify the shirts?"

"I sure can," Soapy said. "I've had them long enough. Size sixteen, all of them. Three white dress shirts and five sports shirts—two blue, two gray, and one red."

"One minute. I'll check it." The clerk opened the package. "Three white shirts. One red. Two gray. Two blue. They all check."

"Excuse me," the stranger said, moving up beside Soapy. "Did you say you lost your laundry ticket?"

Soapy turned in surprise. "Yes, sir, I did."

"That's a coincidence," the man said. "I found one. Let's see if they match." He laid a ticket beside the one on the counter. "How about that! They're the same. Eighty-six, ninety-four."

"They're the same," the clerk agreed.

"That's funny," Soapy said. "Where did you find it?"

"Perhaps I ought to ask the questions," the man replied quietly. He pulled a small leather case out of his pocket and held it up in front of Soapy's eyes. "I'm Detective Gil Minton. City police. I'd like to ask you a few questions. Down at headquarters . . ."

CHAPTER 7

PALM OF HIS HAND

DETECTIVE GIL MINTON drove his black, two-door car swiftly and surely through the evening traffic and parked the car behind the police station. Then he led the way through a rear door and up several flights of stairs to a small room furnished with two tables, several straight-backed chairs, and a wall telephone.

"Have a seat, fellows," he said, moving to the telephone. Lifting the receiver, he spoke into the mouthpiece. "This is Minton. Ask Fred to come up to Room Six, will you, Jim?"

Seconds later, a short, fat man with gray hair entered the room and addressed Minton. "What's up, Gil?"

"The laundry check. This young fellow is Robert Smith. His laundry checks with the lead I've been following."

The newcomer glanced curiously at Soapy. "I see. . . ." Then he glanced at Chip. "And this fellow?"

"He's a friend of Smith's. Chip Hilton, the State basketball star. Fellows, this is Detective Fred Parks."

Chip and Soapy nodded and Detective Minton continued, "Hilton and Smith both go to school here and they both work at State Drug."

Detective Parks sat down behind the table. "How about Hilton? Do we need him?"

"Not necessarily, Fred. He wanted to come."

"All right, it's not important." He turned to Soapy. "Now, Smith, we have to ask you some questions. Detective Minton is going to write down the answers, so think carefully before you answer."

"But what's this all about?" Soapy asked indignantly. "I'm no criminal. I've never been in trouble in my life."

"That's right," Chip added. "We grew up together. I think we ought to be told what you're trying to find out. You don't have to worry about Soapy. He'll tell you everything he knows—about anything!"

"Take it easy, Hilton," Detective Minton said gently. "You'll find out all you need to know in a few minutes. Relax, please."

Detective Parks cleared his throat impatiently. "Now, if everyone will be quiet for a few minutes, we can get this over with. Where were you last Wednesday night, Smith?"

Soapy was obviously worried. He glanced at Chip and hesitated briefly before answering. "I was working at the store. At State Drug."

"Can you drive a car?"

"Yes, sir."

"Do you have a car?"

"No, sir."

"Were you in a car last Wednesday night?"

"No, sir. Oh, wait— That was the night of the Cathedral game. Yes, sir, I was. I borrowed Mitzi

Savrill's car to drive Chip home from the game. He has a bad leg."

"I know. Who is Mitzi Savrill?"

"She's the cashier and bookkeeper at State Drug."

"What's the color of Miss Savrill's car?"

Soapy considered a second. "It has a dark body, blue, and a white top."

The detectives exchanged significant glances. Then Parks continued his interrogation. "What time did you borrow the car?"

"About ten fifteen."

"You drove Hilton home. Then what did you do?"

Soapy hesitated. "Well, I started back to the drug-store—"

"And?"

"And I had a flat tire."

"Where?"

"About three miles out Main Street."

Parks nodded thoughtfully. "What were you doing way out there?"

"I—I was just taking a ride."

"What time was it then?"

Soapy deliberated. "It was about eleven forty."

"You were alone in the car?"

"Yes, sir. That is— Yes, sir."

"What time did you return the car to Miss Savrill?"

"It was about twelve fifteen, sir."

"Now, Smith, did you stop anywhere during those two hours?"

Soapy hesitated again. "No, sir. That is, only when I had the flat tire."

"Did you talk to anyone?"

"Yes, sir. To the fellows who changed the tire."

Detective Parks questioned Soapy in detail about

the exact time the fellows arrived to help him change the tire, who they were, the time they left, and how fast he drove the car back to the restaurant. During the questioning, Detective Minton kept scribbling in his writing pad.

Chip wanted to call State Drug to let them know what had happened but he didn't like to leave Soapy. He was relieved when Detective Parks suggested that they take a little drive. Soapy and Detective Parks got in the back seat and Chip sat in the front with Minton who was driving. Chip was determined to stick with Soapy and find out what it was all about. He wasn't kept long in doubt.

Detective Minton drove rapidly up Main Street and out toward State's campus. Just before the main drive, he turned into the Triangle Service Station and pulled up beside the shop. "This is as far as we go," he said, turning off the motor.

Chip recognized the station and a premonition seized him. *The holdup! Now he knew what it was all about.*

Inside the station, Detective Parks shook hands with the attendant and got right to the point. He waved a hand toward Chip and Soapy. "Recognize either of these fellows, Welsh? Can you identify either one of them?"

"This is ridiculous," Chip said hotly.

"Hold it, Hilton!" Parks said sharply. He turned to the attendant. "Well, Welsh?"

Welsh took off his glasses and wiped them with his handkerchief. Then he ignored Chip and pranced around Soapy like a bantam rooster, looking at the redhead from one side and then the other. He stopped and shook his head uncertainly. Then he put on his glasses and walked around Soapy again.

"Hmm," he said. "About the same size, all right. Red hair, too! And a fat nose. He looks like him, but I can't be sure. Now if he had a brown hat—"

"A hat!" Soapy exploded. "I never wore a hat in my life! And I've only been in this gas station twice in my life. Once with Chip and once last week during the storm."

"That's enough, Smith," Parks said, shaking Soapy's arm. "You be quiet. Well, Welsh?"

The grouchy attendant shook his head uncertainly. "The guy was wearing a hat," he said sullenly. "An old brown hat with—"

"Here!" Detective Parks interrupted, placing his own hat on Soapy's head. "How's that?"

"Well," Welsh drawled reluctantly, "it's not brown and I can't be sure. Now if he only had on an old blue sweater—"

Parks grabbed the hat off Soapy's head and jammed it back on his own head. "Look, Welsh, we can't carry a whole wardrobe around. Is this the fellow or not?"

"Well," Welsh drawled, "as I said, I didn't get a very good look at him, but if you put him in the car over by the last pump and open the window—"

"All right," Parks said patiently. "We'll try that!"

Welsh and Soapy and the two detectives walked out to the car and Chip seized the opportunity to call State Drug. He got Mitzi on the telephone and explained what had happened. "Tell Mr. Grayson, will you, Mitzi? And hurry! Oh, yes, Mitzi—please don't say anything about it to anyone else."

By the time Chip finished the call, the detectives had parked their car by the last pump. Soapy was sitting in the car behind the wheel, leaning out the open window.

"Well," Parks said, turning to Welsh, "now what?"

"Well, it was snowing," Welsh said uncertainly. "And my glasses were all wet."

Detective Minton turned away, shrugging his shoulders. "Now he wants snow!"

"Listen, Welsh," Detective Parks said roughly, "we can't stay here all night. Now I know it was eleven forty-five at night, and it was dark, and your glasses were all clouded up, and the man wore a brown hat, and he had it pulled down over his eyes, and he wore a blue sweater, and you thought he had red hair. . . .

"And when you finished putting the gasoline in the tank, he sneaked up behind you and poked a gun in your back and asked for the money you had in your pocket. And then he made you turn around and told you to go back into the station. And he said he would shoot if you came out before he drove away."

Detective Parks was almost shouting, now. He paused for breath and then said, "Now, for the last time, is this the man?"

Before Welsh could answer, there was an interruption. A taxi careened into the station and slowed down with screeching tires. George Grayson leaped out of the car and hurried toward the group. "What's going on, Chip?" he asked.

"Just a minute—" Parks began roughly. Then he recognized the newcomer. "Oh! Mr. Grayson. I—"

"Hello, Parks, Minton. What's going on here?"

"Give us a second, Mr. Grayson. We'll explain everthing." Parks turned back to Welsh. "All right. Is this the man or not?"

"As I was saying," Welsh persisted, "all these young fellers look alike nowadays and—"

"All right, all right, Welsh," Parks said resignedly. "That's enough."

"Now can I have an explanation?" George Grayson asked.

Parks' attitude was conciliatory but firm. "We're just doing our duty, Mr. Grayson. Undoubtedly you know that we've had a number of gas-station robberies during the last two months. This station was robbed last Wednesday and Smith's laundry check was found here the same night. So we've been asking him a few questions."

"I told you I stopped here for gas that night," Soapy said. "But I didn't rob anyone. That night or any other night."

"Is everything cleared up now?" Grayson asked.

Parks shook his head. "Not quite, sir. You see, Smith admits he was using a car that night which answers the description of the car the bandit was driving. Further, his explanation of his travels that night is vague and unsatisfactory. Besides, there is a discrepancy in time to be accounted for . . . He has told us that he had a flat tire three miles out Main Street and there is cause for considerable conjecture since he can't give us a good reason for being in that vicinity. The flat tire could have happened anywhere. A block from here or several miles away. So far, he hasn't accounted for his whereabouts at eleven forty-five, the exact time of the robbery."

"I can see your position, Parks," Grayson said understandingly, "but from what I've heard, this man's identification is worthless."

"Now you listen here," Welsh began. "I—"

Detective Minton checked Welsh. "We have to start *somewhere*, Mr. Grayson," he said slowly. "If

Smith now would only be a little more specific—"

"But you can't keep the boy out here all night just because you found a laundry ticket. He admits he stopped here for gasoline and he's certainly explained the car satisfactorily."

"That's right, Mr. Grayson, but the other details aren't very clear."

"They can surely wait. I know he will be able to explain everything to your satisfaction when he's had a chance to collect his wits. I'll vouch for him. Suppose we get together tomorrow afternoon in my office. I think we can clear this thing up quickly enough so far as Soapy is concerned."

"All right, Mr. Grayson," Parks said decisively. "That's all right with us."

"I'll vouch for him. I know you fellows both realize it is extremely important to Soapy that all of this be kept confidential. Important to me, too."

"Don't worry about our end," Minton said significantly. "We never give out information on routine investigations. I don't suppose Smith or Hilton are going to do much talking about it."

"You can be sure of that," Grayson said grimly.

Parks turned to Soapy with a brief smile. "Don't leave town, young man."

"Leave town!" Soapy gasped. "Why would I leave town? I like it here. Heck, I'm stayin' here until I graduate from State."

The two detectives drove away and George Grayson headed for the telephone booth inside the building. Chip and Soapy listened to the garrulous chatter of the station attendant while they waited.

"Detectives!" Welsh snorted. "Huh! They couldn't catch a cold." He peered suspiciously at Soapy. "If they had only put a brown hat on your head and got me a blue sweater, I'd have known for sure. You got a brown hat?"

"I never had a hat in my life," Soapy said. "Unless you call a sailor cap a hat. I had my picture taken in one of those when I was two years old."

Welsh grunted sarcastically. "Bein' smart, eh? Won't do you any good to get smart with me. I got you right here." He tapped the palm of his hand. "All I need is a brown hat with a coupla fishin' feathers stuck in the hatband. Green ones!"

"But you haven't identified him," Chip said shortly.

Welsh looked Chip up and down, the expression on his face clearly contemptuous. "Well, now, maybe I have and maybe I haven't, Bub."

"It isn't very well lighted out here at night," Chip countered, "so I don't see how you could identify a person even if he *did* put on a sweater and a brown hat."

"There's nothing wrong with my eyes, young fellow," Welsh blustered.

George Grayson returned then, and the conversation ended. On the way back to State Drug in the taxi, Chip and Soapy filled in the missing parts of the night's adventure. Their employer listened intently, stopping them from time to time to clear up certain details. When the taxi reached State Drug, Mr. Grayson paid the driver and stood beside Chip and Soapy on the sidewalk until he had been told the entire story.

"We'll straighten it out tomorrow afternoon," Grayson said confidently. "Now you had better get back on the job. On second thought, I better go in first. We don't want to attract too much atten-

tion. Suppose you get a cup of coffee at Pete's Place."
He patted Soapy's shoulder. "Now don't worry.
Everything is going to be all right."

The two boys found an empty booth in the little
restaurant and talked it over while they sipped their
coffee. "Some man," Soapy said admiringly. "Boy,
did he take charge!"

"Yes, but I'm worried, Soapy," Chip said. "What
were you doing all that time?"

"I told you I had a flat."

"But what were you doing all the way out Main
Street? Why, you had to go right past the store.
Where were you going?"

"Gee, Chip, what's that got to do with it?"

"Everything. You're under suspicion."

Chip let that sink in and then said, "I know you
wouldn't do anything wrong, Soapy. I've got a hunch
you took Jane Adams home. Right?"

Soapy nodded. "Yes, that's right, Chip."

"Well, why didn't you say so? What's wrong with
taking Jane home? Mitzi would understand that."

"Sure. Sure, I guess so, Chip. I just didn't want
to get Jane involved with Parks and Minton."

They sat without speaking for a long minute, each
thinking of the night's events and its implications.
Chip broke the silence. "The police don't know you
from Adam. And what's more important, you can't
expect them to believe *anything* if you don't tell
them everything. That's logical enough, isn't it?"

"Sure, Chip."

"Do you remember what my mother always said
about telling the truth?"

"Sure I do," Soapy said. " 'Always tell the truth and
you never have to remember what you said.' "

CHAPTER 8

HOLLYWOOD STYLE

LATER THAT NIGHT, after they had gone to bed, Chip began to probe Soapy again. "Soapy," he said gently, "try to get the time element straightened out in your mind. The detectives seem to feel it's important."

"I know, Chip. I am trying."

"What time did you get Jane home?"

"It was exactly eleven twenty-five. Jane checked the time with her wrist watch."

"Did you start right back?"

"Sure. But I didn't get far. That's when I had the flat. About five minutes after I left Jane. And it was about ten minutes before those three fellows came along."

"What time was it then?"

"About eleven forty. And it was eleven fifty-five when they left. I checked that when I got in the car. And it was exactly twelve fifteen when I reached the restaurant."

"That's better," Chip said. "Now stick to that."

There was no sound in the room for a few minutes, but just as Chip was dozing off, Soapy spoke once more. "Chip, you don't think Mitzi will be angry because I took Jane home, do you?"

"I think she would be extremely angry if you hadn't. Me, too! I *do* think you could have stopped at the store and told her where you were going. Now let's get some sleep."

Neither boy got much sleep that night. Chip heard his roommate tossing and turning. In the morning both were dead tired. Soapy was concerned about Chip's knee but avoided further reference to the robbery.

Chip skipped the noon meeting with his pals and took a bus to State Drug to report what he had learned from Soapy. George Grayson was pleased. "I'm glad to hear about Jane," he said. "That clears up a lot of things. You run along now and leave everything to me."

When Chip reported for practice, Murph Kelly gave him a heat treatment and sent him out on the floor to limber up his knee by shooting baskets. Chip didn't benefit much from that practice. Accurate shooting requires absolute concentration and Chip was in no mood to concentrate on anything except Soapy's predicament.

A little later the trainer came up to watch practice and noticed Chip's inaccurate marksmanship. He sauntered down to the practice basket to find out the trouble. "What's the matter, Chip? Is your knee bothering you?"

"No, Murph, something else. Do you mind if I call it a day?"

"Mind? What do you think? Beat it!"

Chip dressed quickly and caught a downtown bus. A block before the State Drug corner, Chip hustled out of the bus and up to the front entrance of the store. Then he sauntered slowly through the door and up to the cashier's desk. On the way he glanced at the fountain. Soapy was not in sight.

"Hello, Chip," Mitzi said gently. "Mr. Grayson wants to see you. He's in his office."

"Where's Soapy?"

"Mr. Grayson sent him around to Pete's Place to eat. He had a pretty long afternoon."

"Are they gone?"

Mitzi nodded. "Just a few minutes ago. They looked at the car and asked me about letting Soapy use it. I guess they are satisfied."

"I'm sure glad to hear that. Thanks, Mitzi."

Ann Tracy was typing busily when Chip entered the reception office. She smiled and nodded her head toward the inner office. "Go right in, Chip. Mr. Grayson is expecting you."

George Grayson looked up and nodded toward a vacant chair. "Well, so far, so good. I told Parks and Minton about Jane and they talked to her and she verified that part of Soapy's story."

Chip breathed a sigh of relief. "Then everything is all right—"

"Not quite. Parks and Minton claim Soapy could have taken Jane home and still have gotten back to the station by eleven forty-five. Soapy isn't going to be in the clear until they locate the fellows who helped him with the tire and verify the time. By the way, I sent Soapy down to Pete's Place. Why don't you drop down there and talk to him?"

Soapy was sitting in a rear booth at the restaurant eating a sandwich when Chip slid into the opposite seat. He looked up in surprise. "Chip! What's wrong? Didn't you go to practice?"

"Sure I went to practice."

"Is your knee worse?"

"No, it's all right. What happened?"

"Well, they asked a lot of questions and talked to Mitzi and Jane, and looked at the car. But they didn't seem to be satisfied about the flat tire."

"How do you know?"

"I could tell by the questions. Parks would say: 'Now, Smith, put yourself in my place. Wouldn't you think it strange if I told you that three fellows came along in a car and helped me out of a lot of trouble and I didn't even ask their names, or remember what they looked like, or where they lived, or noticed the kind of car they were driving?'

"And I said, 'Yes, sir, Mr. Parks, I would.'

"Then Minton would say: 'I don't understand how you can be so sure about the exact time you picked up Miss Adams and the exact time you had the flat tire and the exact time they got the spare on the car and the exact time you reached State Drug. It's just *too* exact.'"

"What did you say to that?"

"I told him it was all a coincidental—"

"Coincidence."

"Well, a series of coincidents. Just like the stuff about the laundry ticket and the car and the time was circumstantial."

"Then what?"

"Well, they both laughed and Minton said something about a lot of double-talk. Then they sobered up and said they were going to concentrate on finding the three guys."

"Was that all?"

Soapy grinned derisively. "All? Sure! That's all— all I heard for three hours."

"Three hours!" Chip echoed. "No wonder you're

down. Well, come on, we'll be through work in three hours. Then we're going straight home and sit down and figure out how to locate those three fellows."

Immediately after work he and Soapy took a bus to Jeff and were in their room at ten forty-five. Chip went right to work.

"Now why didn't you get the names of those fellows?"

"Gee, Chip, it was snowing a wet snow. And we were all soaking wet. No one wanted to talk."

"Couldn't you see their faces?"

"Sure, but I didn't pay any attention."

"Which one did the most talking?"

"Well, the tall fellow, I guess."

"How tall? How heavy?"

"Aw, Chip, how do I know. You're worse than Parks and Minton. He was about six-three or four, I guess. About a hundred and ninety pounds."

"You must have noticed something else. A ring or a watch or glasses, or—"

Soapy leaped to his feet. "Yeah, that's it! He was wearin' glasses. They were cloudy and he kept saying he couldn't see without them and he couldn't see with them."

"What kind of clothes was he wearing?"

"Aw, Chip, I told you it was snowing and then raining. How could I tell what he had on? Besides, he was wearing a raincoat."

"What kind of raincoat? Cheap? Good?"

"It was a good one, all right."

"Now, how about his features?"

"He had a long nose," Soapy said wearily, dropping back on his pillow.

"What kind of lips? Thin or full?"

Soapy sat up suddenly and jerked the drawer of

his desk open. "Hey! I've got an idea. You're good at drawing. Right? Why don't you draw a picture of the guy?" He tossed a notebook to Chip and stretched out on the bed once more. "O.K., now, let's have the questions."

"I'm not that good."

"Yes, you are. Try it."

Chip began to sketch the outline of a face, carefully drawing in the nose and the mouth. "What about the eyes? Remember the color?"

"You kidding? In that weather? All I know is, he had eyes."

"How about the eyebrows and eyelashes?"

"He had bushy eyebrows. Oh, yes. He had black hair. His hat fell off accidentally."

"Crew cut?"

"No, wore his hair Hollywood style. That's why I noticed it."

Chip grunted. "Good. Now we're getting somewhere."

Soapy got up and looked over Chip's shoulder. "Hey! That's perfect. That's him!"

Chip laughed. "It can't be that good."

"But it is. What are you going to do with it?"

"I don't know exactly. But at least I know about what he looks like."

"Boy!" Soapy said admiringly, picking up the paper. "It's just like one of those cartoons they run in the paper."

Chip banged the desk with his fist. "That's it! The papers! We'll run an ad in the papers."

"An ad? What for?"

"For the three fellows."

Soapy nodded thoughtfully. Then his face lit up like a neon light. "You've got it!" he said enthusiastically. "We'll offer a reward. Boy, that's smart!"

"All right, how does this sound? Listen . . .

"Important! Will the three fellows who helped a stranger change a tire last Wednesday night on West Main Street at approximately eleven forty-five P.M. please write to box such-and-such in care of this newspaper. Reward."

Soapy was exuberant. "Sounds great. This is getting interesting." His face sobered. "But suppose those fellows don't see it?"

"Then we'll try something else. Now we're going to bed. Tomorrow's a big day."

"And how! You playing against Mercer tomorrow night?"

"I sure am. I'm going to make the Western trip, too. It will sure be a relief to get away from all this cold weather."

"I'll say. Gee, you'll have a swell time. Those big planes sure eat up the distance. Imagine! All the way out to Oregon and then down to California and back here in just four days!" Soapy's enthusiasm suddenly disappeared and his brow furrowed as he turned out the light. "You gonna be able to play two days in a row, Chip?"

"Sure. I'm through babying my knee. Pleasant dreams, Soapy."

Chip didn't do any dreaming that night. He wished he hadn't said anything about the trip. "Fine thing," he breathed, rebuking himself bitterly. "You go away on the best trip of the year and your best friend stays behind up to his ears in trouble. Some loyalty . . ."

Despite his sleepless night, Chip was the first to waken Wednesday morning. And for the second day in a row, Soapy neglected to rush out for the *News*.

On the way to their first class, Soapy mentioned it. "You know, Chip," he said wryly, "Jim Locke's column has suddenly become *extremely* unimportant."

"That's what I've been trying to tell you all along," Chip said quietly. "And that reminds me. I've got to put the ad in the papers. See you this afternoon."

"How about lunch?"

"I won't have time."

"I guess I'll skip it, too," Soapy said thoughtfully. "I've got to hit the books."

Chip carried the picture of Soapy's worried face in his mind's eye all day, in every class, and in the advertising offices of the *News* and the *Herald*.

And that night in the game with Mercer, Chip forgot all about his knee. He was tired physically but he pushed himself savagely and recklessly, cutting and driving and hustling as if he had never heard of a strained ligament. He was awkward and stiff but he hit for thirty-five points in the thirty minutes he played. State won by a score of 83 to 77.

It was the third win in a row for the Statesmen and Chip's teammates were riding high again. In the dressing room, while Murph Kelly was working on Chip's knee, the gang really cut loose.

"Yippee!" Thornhill yelped, snapping King with his towel. "A little summer weather for a change."

"Three in a row!" Biz Gowdy cried.

"Thanks to Chip," King said, grabbing the towel out of Thornhill's hands.

"Thirty-five points!" Jimmy Lu Chung cried excitedly.

"Now we're rolling," Markley shouted from the shower. "California, here we come!"

CHAPTER 9

TOP OF THE MARK

MITZI SAVRILL drove Chip and Speed and Soapy to the University Airport early Thursday morning. It had snowed during the night and the roads were still icy. Snow was piled high along the sides of the street and sidewalks. It was a long walk from the parking lot to the terminal and the cold wind cut through to the bone. Inside, the players and fans were moving excitedly about. Mitzi contrived to get a few words alone with Chip, suggesting to Soapy that it would be nice to get some newspapers so that the fellows might have something to read.

As soon as Soapy turned away, Mitzi grasped Chip by the arm and led him a few paces away from the crowd. "Don't worry about Soapy while you're gone, Chip. Mr. Grayson said to tell you he would take care of everything." She smiled up at Chip reassuringly. "And I'll help. Soapy is one of the nicest fellows I have ever known."

"He thinks you're pretty wonderful, too," Chip said, smiling down at the efficient little charmer. "Oh, by the way, perhaps you can do something about Fireball and Whitty. They're kidding the life out of Soapy about the car. We haven't told them about his trouble with the police."

"I'll take care of *that*," Mitzi said firmly.

Soapy came rushing back with an armful of papers and magazines just then. "These ought to hold you all the way to Oregon," the redhead said happily, looking from Chip to Mitzi and back again. "Hey," he continued suspiciously, "what have you two been talking about?"

Chip grinned fondly. "Aren't your ears burning?"

Soapy shook his head uncertainly and rubbed his ear. "Uh, uh. Not a bit."

"Well, they ought to be," Chip said, adding hastily, "but it was all good."

The loud-speaker buzzed and the broadcaster announced the departure of Flight Six for Chicago and the West. "Passengers will please board the plane through Gate Four."

"That's us," Speed said, joining the trio. "We're on our way."

Murph Kelly identified the players as they passed through the gate and they hustled toward the plane, anxious to get seats by the windows. Chip paused as he started up the steps. Soapy and Mitzi were standing beside the fence waving good-by and he waved in return.

The big ship carried ninety-six passengers and the seats were arranged with three on one side of the aisle and two on the other. Chip and Speed found two beside a window and peered out. Soapy and Mitzi were still standing beside the railing, scanning the windows of the plane.

In a few minutes every seat was filled and a little later the plane rumbled down the runway to the take-off strip. After a brief pause they were airborne so smoothly that Chip couldn't tell when they had left the ground.

It was a smooth and fast flight to Chicago. Chip closed his eyes to rest and Speed read the papers. They landed at Chicago with scarcely a tremor. In a few minutes the seats of the debarking passengers were filled and the plane took off once again.

The chief hostess of the ship welcomed the new passengers when they leveled off and briefed them on precautionary and safety regulations. A short time later all three hostesses served lunch. Chip enjoyed the flight immensely, although nothing was visible through the window except the big, lazy clouds. Except for the steady roar of the plane, Chip felt as though it was suspended in the sky.

The plane was warm and cozy and Chip was dozing when the captain announced they would be landing in Denver in a few minutes and that the State basketball team would disembark. "The crew and I wish you good luck," he said heartily. "If we're lucky, we may get to see you play Saturday night in the Cow Palace."

The gang liked that and gave the crew a big hand. Then the plane began its swift descent. It broke through the clouds and down below the city of Denver came swiftly into view, completely covered with snow. Chip and Speed were looking out their window when the plane eased down onto the runway, between two high banks of snow that towered above the wings of the ship.

"Where's that warm weather you were talking about, Randy?" Butcher King yelled. "This is worse than University. We'd better get some snowshoes!"

"A guy needs skis in this country," someone retorted.

It was as bad as it looked. A narrow tunnel led through the high banks of snow and they floundered along, yelping, shouting and kidding. But they were glad to get inside the airport building and out of the cold. Murph Kelly had directed them to bring coats and sweaters but the cold still bit through.

Thirty minutes later they tramped back through the snow and boarded a small twenty-eight passenger plane which carried them to Salem, the capital of Oregon. They scoffed at the bus which carried them over the snowbound roads to Gilbert, but most of them were glad to get back on terra firma. Coach Corrigan gave them the evening off and most of the players went to the movies. Chip remained in his room to study and rest his leg.

Friday dawned bright and sunny and warm. Corrigan held a brief skull session and then they were taken on a motor tour of the Gilbert environs by enthusiastic sports fans.

The game that night was hard fought all the way, but State led at the end to win by a score of 66 to 64. Chip was needed in the final two periods. His thirty-one points were high for both teams.

Saturday and Sunday were two of the most interesting days of Chip's life. The flight down the coast to San Francisco was made at ten thousand feet and the shore line was clearly visible all the way. The drive from the airport to the city led past the Cow Palace. Located ten miles from the center of the city in a small industrial section, it seemed a strange setting for a sports arena.

Chip forgot all about that when he learned that Murph Kelly had instructed the taxi drivers to make a short tour. He became absorbed in the interesting scenes of the great city—Grant Street, the heart of the city's Chinatown; world-renowned Nob Hill; the Powell Street cable cars; Fisherman's Wharf; Joe Di Maggio's Restaurant; Market Street and Telegraph Hill. Later, Murph Kelly led them through San Francisco's fabulous shopping center, slowing his progress so Chip could keep pace.

The big thrill came when Kelly engaged a string of taxis and announced that he had arranged a trip to the Top of the Mark. The elevators shot swiftly upward, and they were led to tables beside the floor-to-ceiling windows. Below was the breath-taking skyline view of San Francisco and the Bay.

The international port stretched out below them with shipyards; anchored vessels; Alcatraz, the escapeproof prison for dangerous criminals; famous Treasure Island, used as a Far East debarking point for the Armed Forces in World War II; Golden Gate Bridge, and many other wonderful sights.

Chip was enthralled by the sights but not to the extent that he forgot his best friend. His heart took a sharp dip as he thought how much Soapy would have enjoyed all these wonders. The thought dampened his spirits and he was glad when they started back to the hotel to rest.

The Statesmen taxied to the scene of the game that night. San Francisco's famed Cow Palace turned out to be just what the name implied—an arena constructed for the judging and exhibiting of fine cattle. But it could be converted into a fine all-around sports center. That evening, the basketball court had been placed in the center of the show ring. There was room for seats between the court and the circular wall of the amphitheater but it had not been utilized. About ten thousand spectators were jammed into the arena by game time.

State's opponents, College of the West, was rated
as one of the nation's top teams. The Westerners had
lost to Templeton in the Holiday Invitational Tournament by a score of 52 to 49. Then State and Templeton had battled right down to the wire in the
semifinals, with the Statesmen emerging the winner.
Chip had been injured on an attempted shot just as
the buzzer sounded, ending the game. Then, barely
able to stand, he had dropped in a pair of free
throws to win the game by the narrow margin of one
point, 76 to 75.

This was the same kind of game. A nip-and-tuck
affair. The lead changed hands with almost every
score, and the fans were on their feet cheering the
brilliant performance of both teams right down to
the last play of the game.

Coach Corrigan used Chip sparingly, trying to
protect and rest him, yet win the game. With College
of the West leading 94 to 92 and twenty seconds left
to play, Jimmy Lu Chung dribbled around his opponent and hit with a desperate two-pointer to tie
the score.

On the out-of-bounds play, on Western's pass in
court, Jimmy pulled the old dummy act, pivoting
just in time to deflect the ball. The intended receiver
and Jimmy dove for the ball at the same instant. The
referee called it a held ball when the mad scramble
ended and lined up the two players for the jump.
Jimmy's opponent was a head taller and it was almost certain that he would control the tap.

Speed Morris became the hero, then, taking a des-
perate chance. As the official tossed up the ball,
Speed timed it just right, streaked in front of the
Westerner's big center and intercepted the ball.
Markley immediately called for a time-out.

There were four seconds left to play, the score was tied at 94–94, and every fan in the Cow Palace was on his feet. In the huddle, Corrigan told them to set up their "box" out-of-bounds formation and to work the block so Chip would get the final shot. The buzzer sounded and Markley took the ball out of bounds.

Chip was in the outside corner position of the box, and when Markley slapped the ball, he broke out of his position and cut around the block. Kirk's pass was fast and sure and Chip's fifteen-foot jump shot ripped through the cords just as the final buzzer ended the game. The score: State 96, College of the West, 94.

Chip's thirty-eight points were high for the night, but they were expensive tallies. He could scarcely walk off the court. Murph Kelly helped him to the dressing room, growling angrily on the way. And while the Statesmen celebrated the concluding victory of their Western trip, the veteran trainer worked grimly on Chip's knee.

Sunday was a long, boring day and Chip was relieved when they boarded the plane for home. He leaned back in the reclining seat, tired and worried. It had been a wonderful trip and great to win, but he belonged back in University with Soapy.

Chip was sleeping soundly when the hostess shook his shoulder. "We will be landing in University in a few minutes," she said. "Fasten your seat belt, please."

Chip tightened his belt and peered down at the snow-covered ground which was flying swiftly past. University was coming into view. Chip glanced at his watch. It was exactly seven o'clock.

When the plane glided to a stop in front of the airport, the players headed for the door, their fatigue forgotten. It was good to be back, to be back home with two tough games under their belts, and five straight wins behind them.

Waiting in his seat while his teammates filed out of the plane, Chip looked out the window. Soapy and Mitzi were waiting beyond the exit gates. "I might have known," he muttered. "I hope they have good news."

Soapy was beaming when Chip approached, but Mitzi's solemn expression was foreboding. "Nice going, Chipper," the redhead cried. "Your knee all right?"

"I'm O.K., Soapy. Hello, Mitzi. Any news?"

"Not yet," Mitzi replied glumly.

"Sure there's news!" Soapy said quickly, pulling a paper out of his pocket. "Look at this! In the *News*, no less—" He pointed to the headline and read it aloud:

"'Hilton stars on State's victorious road trip.' Great, eh?"

"That isn't the kind of news I meant. What about the ad?"

Soapy turned quickly away. "There's the baggage truck. I'll grab your bag. Be right back."

Mitzi grasped Chip's arm as soon as Soapy was out of hearing. "Let's wait inside. It's too cold out here."

"Sure, Mitzi. What about the ad?"

"No one has answered so far, Chip."

"They will," Chip said confidently.

"Well, maybe," Mitzi said uncertainly, "but they had better hurry."

"Why?"

"Well, the man at the gas station has changed his mind. He now says Soapy is the bandit!"

CHAPTER 10

WORD OF HONOR

GEORGE GRAYSON leaned back in his chair and shook his head worriedly. "But it isn't circumstantial evidence, Chip. It's a positive identification."

"But Welsh couldn't identify Soapy that first time. What makes him so sure now?"

"I don't know. Parks and Minton are worried about this new development because it puts them on a spot. However, I checked the dates of several of the earlier robberies and a redheaded fellow answering Welsh's general description held up the City Service Station the same night you fellows won the tournament at Clinton."

"Soapy was in Clinton," Chip said quickly. "The whole team could testify to that."

George Grayson nodded. "There's no question about that and it's got them stumped. But Welsh is pressing for action and we've got to act fast. We've got to find those three fellows."

Chip got to his feet. "How much time do we have?"

"That I don't know. But I do know that Parks and Minton have got to move. They're not completely sold on Welsh's identification, but they have to keep after Soapy until he's completely in the clear."

"They've been giving him a bad time all right," Chip said ruefully.

"Did Soapy tell you that?"

"No, sir. But I know Soapy about as well as I know myself, I guess. Anyway, every time I mentioned the ad he changed the subject."

Grayson nodded. "Soapy would do that. Chip, we've got one serious problem. If Welsh begins to talk and raise a fuss, we're all going to be on the spot. Parks, Minton, you, me—everyone concerned."

"I can understand that, sir."

"This robbery is probably the only sensational thing Welsh ever experienced," Grayson said. "He would probably identify *me* as the robber if he thought he could get his picture in the paper."

"There's not much doubt of that, sir."

"And," George Grayson continued thoughtfully, "if some reporter like Jim Locke—if there *is* another reporter like him—should hear Welsh's story, Soapy's picture would be plastered all over the front page."

That brought the danger right out in the open and Chip thoughtfully considered the import of the words. What to do? . . .

George Grayson interrupted Chip's thoughts. "I'm behind Soapy all the way. I'm sure you are aware of that. But we *must* find those three fellows. If there is any way I can help, count on me. I don't want to be trite, but I'm as close as your telephone. Here at the store or at home."

Chip forgot all about school, basketball, State

Drug and everything else except Soapy's problem. He spent the rest of the morning in the stockroom trying to think of a new angle. But he arrived at only one important conclusion: he needed help and he could no longer keep Soapy's secret from the rest of their pals.

Chip took the bus back to the campus and found Soapy eating lunch in the Student Union restaurant. He told Soapy about advising their pals about the robbery and was relieved when the redhead gave his approval. Then he started back downtown.

Pete's Place was practically empty when Chip stopped in for a cup of coffee and a sandwich. After serving him, Pete brought over a copy of the *Herald*.

"Nice shooting, Chip. Bill Bell gives you a big plug here in the paper. Listen: 'Chip Hilton's sensational hoop scoring under fire proves his national marksmanship title is not a stand-around, practice-shot crown.' O.K.?

" 'Hilton has scored four hundred and twenty-one points in three hundred and thirty-three minutes of play to give the "Dead-Eye Dick" an average of one and three-tenth points per minute and slightly over thirty-two points per game.'

"How's that? And listen to this: 'The National Marksmanship Tournament has caught on all over the country and Chip Hilton's crown will be the goal of the greatest list of sharpshooters in the history of the event. The local A.A.U. office has been swamped by entries for the State finals to be held here on February eleven and twelve—'

"All right, eh? Hey, what's the matter, pal? You sick?"

"No, I'm all right, Pete. Just worried, that's all."

"You're worried! How about Corrigan and the fans and everyone else around here? We're just as worried about that knee as you are."

"It's not my knee, Pete. It's something a lot more important."

"This I gotta hear. What is it?"

Chip pulled a piece of paper out of his pocket and checked Pete's name off the list. Then, after extracting a promise of secrecy, he told Pete about Soapy's predicament. Pete was flabbergasted.

"Can't be! Why—why it's impossible! Soapy wouldn't steal a toothpick. What can I do to help?"

"I don't know, Pete. That's why I thought I would call a meeting of all of Soapy's friends and try to figure out something."

Pete nodded approval. "That's what I call teamwork. Too many cooks don't *always* spoil the broth. You can count on me. Jimmy, too! How about holding the meeting right here? We'll close at eleven o'clock and pull the blinds. O.K.?"

"Great! You tell Jimmy. I'll get word to everyone else."

"What about training rules? I thought you were s'posed to be home by eleven o'clock."

"I can get a late permission from Murph Kelly. I'll see you at eleven o'clock."

Chip left the restaurant and hurried down Main Street toward police headquarters. On the way he thought about the kindly detective who had helped him straighten out some of Eddie Redding's problems. Lieutenant Byrnes, director of University's Police Athletic League program, was a real friend of youngsters. Chip found the detective at his desk and plunged right into the problem. Byrnes knew Soapy and was generally familiar with the case. He listened attentively while Chip detailed Soapy's travels on the disastrous night.

"Mr. Parks and Mr. Minton have been giving him a pretty rough time."

"Smith is having quite an ordeal, Chip. But Fred and Gil are up against it, too.

"You see, Chip, a detective is in a little different position than a police officer. A police officer is given a regular assignment, called a beat, and his duties are more or less routine. Other officers, usually sergeants and lieutenants, drive what we call prowl cars. They, too, are assigned to certain areas and keep in touch with headquarters by means of their car radios.

"Now a detective, often called a plain-clothes man, may be assigned to a certain area or he may be placed in charge of a certain case or a number of cases. It's up to these men to follow all leads, shadow suspects, set up the machinery of identification through fingerprinting, question principals, and all others who may have some knowledge of the case for information which will help solve it. It's a tough job."

"I know, Lieutenant. Soapy realizes that, too. But they've got him worried sick by the questioning and Welsh's identification."

Byrnes nodded. "That's understandable. The big difficulty with respect to Smith is the identification by that fellow Welsh. That puts Fred and Gil right on the spot. They can't take a single thing for granted. They have to follow through on every angle. If something serious like a shooting should occur and they failed to cover every possibility, they probably would be reduced in rank and might even lose their jobs."

"But I've known Soapy all my life—"

"But they haven't, Chip."

"Well, I know that Soapy couldn't do anything wrong."

"There again Fred and Gil don't know. The impossible seems to be the rule in many of the cases they solve. Some people who become involved in crime are unable to recall any part of it, cases of amnesia, temporary insanity, and all sorts of mental lapses. It could happen to Smith or— Now, let me see the drawing."

Detective Byrnes studied the drawing carefully. "Not bad," he said, tapping the paper with his finger. "We have an artist do the same thing when we have no photograph to go on. This isn't bad at all. What else are you doing?"

"That's about it."

"Perhaps I can help. I can have our mug bureau —that's our identification department—run off thirty or forty copies of this sketch and you can hand them out to your friends. Drop back around seven o'clock this evening. I'll put a rush order on it and the man on the night desk will have them."

Back at State Drug, Chip called Murph Kelly and received permission to skip practice. Then he took the bus to the campus and contacted the rest of his pals. Speed put in a hurried call to the trainer and came back smiling. That evening, when Soapy reported for work, Chip's plans were all set. He had seen Lieutenant Byrnes and had a sheaf of sketches. And when Pete Thorp and Jimmy Lu Chung pulled down the restaurant blinds at eleven o'clock that night, it looked like a Valley Falls reunion.

Biggie Cohen, Fats Ohlson, Tug Rankin, Red Schwartz, Speed Morris, Soapy, and Chip made up the home-town gang, and Fireball Finley, Phil Whittemore, Pete Thorp, and Jimmy Lu Chung were the adopted members. Chip explained the purpose of the meeting and what had been done. Then he waited for suggestions.

Biggie cracked a table with his massive fist. "I ought to go out there and pin that gas-station guy's ears back," he said angrily, squaring his big shoulders. "I know it sounds silly but that's the way I feel."

"How about setting up a night watch on some gas stations?" Schwartz asked.

"That's a thought," Fireball said quickly. "It gives me an idea, too. Why couldn't this gas-station guy have yelled cops-and-robbers and kept the money?"

"He's a peculiar fellow, Fireball," Chip said, smiling. "But I don't think he has that much imagination."

"Maybe not," Biggie said. "But anyone who would identify an innocent person as a thief is capable of anything."

Red Schwartz ventured that there were only a few gas stations open after ten o'clock and that they could easily cover them. The thief was bound to try another stick-up.

"How about talking to this Welsh?" Whittemore asked. "Maybe we could make him change his mind about Soapy."

"Parks and Minton wouldn't like that," Chip said. "Besides, it would probably antagonize the fellow. Goodness knows what he *would* do if he thought we were trying to influence him."

"You can say that again," Soapy muttered.

At the conclusion of the meeting, Chip passed out the sketch prints and they all agreed to help man the service-station night watches. Chip was to make the assignments. Then Pete served coffee "on the house" and drove the Jeff crowd home.

Tuesday was the beginning of a long, hard week for Chip. Preparing for the mid-terms was especially difficult because Chip found it hard to concentrate. He staggered through, though, and then made up the watch lists. Then, he called on Lieutenant Byrnes. The detective was not very enthusiastic about the night-watch plan, but he gave Chip several emergency telephone numbers to call and advised him not to play a policeman's role.

"The sketch idea is fine, Chip. But trying to catch a thief red-handed is something else. I admire your determination, but it's dangerous. For the time being, I suggest you confine the watches to the service stations near the campus.

"If you or any of your pals see someone acting suspiciously, call one of the telephone numbers I gave you and let us handle the situation. Try to get a good description of the fellow, his car, the car's license number, and note the time. But let us do the rest. Remember, Chip, a holdup man with a gun often loses his head. And when he does, well, someone usually gets hurt. Be sure to make it clear to the rest of your pals that they're merely trying to get information.

"Oh, I nearly forgot. I'll see that your crowd gets a little protection." He paused and smiled. "As you know, we patrol the campus area pretty carefully."

After leaving Lieutenant Byrnes, Chip called Murph Kelly on the telephone and requested another late permission. Kelly was reluctant. "How about your treatments?" he demanded.

"They'll have to wait, Murph."

Kelly grunted. "Well, at least you've got sense enough to rest. About time! See you tomorrow afternoon."

Chip took the Triangle station watch that night. Biggie Cohen and Speed Morris were assigned to the City and the Main Street stations. Hopefully excited, Chip slipped into the shadows across from the gas station. But as the minutes ticked away and the cold wind bit through the light overcoat he was wearing, his enthusiasm waned. It was a long, bitter evening. Few cars stopped at the station and he breathed a sigh of relief when Welsh closed up and drove away.

Chip was out on his feet when he got home. Soapy was asleep, but the redhead was far from enjoying his slumber. He turned and tossed and murmured all night. Chip was up at five o'clock the next morning, hitting the books, boning up for his Latin test. Soapy joined him a little later and spoke scarcely a word. Both were concerned about the mid-terms.

When Chip limped into the dressing room that afternoon, Murph Kelly greeted him grumpily. After he examined Chip's knee he was grouchier than ever. "No practice for you," he said gruffly. "Now get out of here and don't come back until Friday noon."

That was a break for Chip. The bad knee and Soapy's trouble had taken his mind off his studies, and now that mid-terms were right around the corner, every minute he could devote to boning up was important.

Red Schwartz, Jimmy Lu Chung, and Fats Ohlson covered the Wednesday and Thursday watches with no results. But Pete Thorp had been busy. He had distributed the sketch prints to his friends around town. Chip waited expectantly, hoping that the missing men would turn up. But nothing happened. And every day, as he watched Soapy's spirits drop, Chip became more determined.

Before it seemed possible, it was Friday, mid-terms were over, and it was nearly time for Chip to report for the two-day trip on which archrivals A. & M. and Southern would be met.

Chip waited for Soapy in the library, caught between two fires: loyalty to the team and a fierce

Chip slipped into the shade

desire to remain beside his pal. But Soapy took care
of that situation.

"You can't let the team down, Chip. They need
your help. And don't forget—A. & M. is the biggest
game on the schedule. This year or any year.

"I know what's in your mind, Chip. But I can
take care of myself. I just won't stand for you letting
the team down because of me. Nothing is going to
happen around here in two days that hasn't already
happened."

cross from the gas station

Now, sitting on the rubbing table while Murph Kelly and Dr. Terring examined his knee, Chip half hoped he would be left behind. Then he saw the tense faces of his teammates as they stood by, anxiously awaiting the decision, and he knew Soapy was right. He belonged with the team.

"It doesn't look too bad," Dr. Terring said, turning to the trainer. "What do you think, Murph?"

Kelly shook his head uncertainly. "I don't know, Doc. You can't tell much by looking at a ligament. We just have to go by what Chip tells us."

"That isn't very much," Terring concluded.

"But it always feels the same," Chip said quickly. "Whether I play or not. And the brace is wonderful. It holds my knee real tight."

"Sure," Kelly rasped. "Sure it does. Why wouldn't it?"

"I'll tell Coach when it's bothering me, Doc," Chip promised. "Word of honor."

"We've got to win these two games," Markley said.

"He'll help just sitting on the bench," Randy Thornhill chimed in. "Right, gang?"

The responding chorus from the players left little doubt of their feelings, and Terring shook his head resignedly. "All right, Hilton. But I'm holding you to your promise. Remember—word of honor!"

CHAPTER 11

TRUTH WILL OUT

TRADITIONAL RIVALS and natural rivals are not always synonymous. But where State and A. & M. were concerned, both terms meant the same thing. A victory for either school in any sport meant a successful season and was a sure guarantee that the coach of the winning team would be back for another season.

A. & M. had won the conference title the previous year and was well on her way to a successful defense of the championship. The Farmers had won fourteen and lost but two games so far, and nine of the victories had been in conference competition. On the debit side of the ledger, there was nothing but a big goose egg.

The two-hundred-mile bus ride from University to Archton was not much of a trip. But most of the Statesmen were weary when they reached the Aggie Hotel. After a light pregame meal, Murph Kelly made them "hit the sack."

But that night, when the Statesmen lined up against their archrivals at eight thirty, they were fresh, confident, and determined to win. Chip sat out the first quarter as his teammates held their own, matching the Farmers point for point. But in the second quarter, when A. & M. began to forge ahead to lead by 26 to 20, Corrigan sent Chip in for Randy Thornhill. The Aggie fans gave Chip a tremendous hand. But he couldn't do much. His knee was as stiff as a board, and, before he could get going, the half ended with A. & M. leading by a score of 30 to 21.

Coach Corrigan tried to protect Chip again in the third quarter. But A. & M. broke loose with a nine-point splurge to lead by fifteen points, and he had no alternative but to try everything in the book. He revised his line-up and sent the Statesmen into their zone press.

The Farmers were ready for State's famous Holiday Tournament strategy, but they couldn't cope with the accurate shooting of Jimmy Lu Chung, Speed Morris, Sky Bollinger, Reb Tucker, and Chip. The wide-open scramble gave Chip more than enough time to get set, and his long shots rippled the cords with deadly precision.

In the final seconds of the game, the Farmers assigned two men to play Chip all over the court. That left one man unguarded and it turned out to be Jimmy. The Statesmen located him immediately and hit the dribbling wizard with the ball. Jimmy was all alone under the basket when he scored the winning field goal to put State ahead at the final buzzer, 72 to 71. Chip got twenty-eight points during the twenty-two minutes he played.

It was a great win for State and the dressing-room celebration was reminiscent of the scene following the tournament victory.

Chip felt good when he went to bed that night.

But the next morning every step brought a streak
of pain from his ankle to his thigh. He covered up
as best he could and kept the pain to himself. Or
at least he thought he did. But later, after the
bus trip to Southern, Murph Kelly appeared in the
room Chip was sharing with Speed, and worked on
his knee for nearly an hour.

"Who do you think you're kidding?" Kelly demanded. "Remember your promise."

"But it didn't hurt while I was playing."

"Just the same, if it isn't any better tonight, you
tell Coach. You hear?"

That night, while he was warming up, Chip saw
Kelly and Coach Corrigan watching him closely.
When the game started he was on the bench and
he remained there all through the first half. It was a
slow, control-ball contest, just the type of game
State's veterans handled best.

Midway in the third period, Southern moved out
in front and Coach Corrigan called for a time-out.
"How about it, Chip? Are you all right?"

Chip leaped to his feet. "Sure! Yes, sir!"

Corrigan eyed him warily, then nodded. "All right.
But you let me know. . . . Report for Thornhill."

Corrigan's slow attack eliminated a lot of the sudden starts, stops, and change-of-direction slants
State's pressure attack required, but Chip found the
slow movements were more than he could maintain.
But he kept trying and managed to score four long
set shots to put State two points ahead. Then, for
the first time since his injury in the tournament, he
said "Uncle." He had gone as far as he could go.

As soon as State got the ball, Chip asked Markley
to call for a time-out. When the referee signaled,
Chip walked slowly to the bench. "I'm sorry, Coach,"

he said. "I guess you had better take me out."

Murph Kelly sat down beside him and loosened the brace. "I'm glad you did the right thing," he growled.

State's veterans held the two-point lead, keeping the ball until they got their shots. On the defense, they played a tight man-to-man defense and lasted it out. The final score: State 65, Southern 63.

The next morning the bus took them back to University. It was three o'clock when they reached Jeff. Fats Ohlson and Biggie Cohen saw Chip and Speed from the reading room and hurried out to help them with their bags. They were buzzing with excitement.

"The whole campus is talking about last night. Nice going! What an upset!"

"Where's Soapy?" Chip asked.

"He went out early this morning," Biggie told him worriedly. "We've got to do something about this thing fast, Chip. It's getting him down."

"Any news?"

"Nope, not a thing."

"I'm going down to Pete's. If you see Soapy, tell him I'll wait there until six o'clock."

Jimmy Lu Chung was on the job when Chip reached the restaurant. He brought Chip a malted milk and the Sunday papers. "Locke again," he said laconically, opening the *News*. "Read that third paragraph."

Chip read the paragraph aloud. " 'Lack of practice seems to have little effect upon the shooting accuracy of State's leading scorer. Particularly on the team's road trips. This reporter attended four State practices this past week and Chip Hilton was absent each time. It must be gratifying, even to a star of Hilton's magnitude, to relax during the strenuous practice sessions and then show up in time to star in the interesting road games.'"

"Well?" Jimmy demanded.

"I'm used to it, Jimmy."

"I'll never get used to that guy. Oh! Tech won again. Number thirteen. That's a lucky number."

"I guess it's about as lucky as unlucky. By the way, where's Pete?"

"He took off as soon as I came in."

"Anything new on the sketch?"

"Nothing much. Pete's been busy, though. He's got that sketch plastered all over town."

Jimmy went back to work and Chip opened the *Herald* to the sports section. There was a story of the Southern game on the first page and a schedule of the Marksmanship Tournament. Chip read both and then turned the page. A banner streamer extended across the top of page two.

UNDEFEATED POLY-TECH RACKS UP NUMBER THIRTEEN

ENGINEERS EXTEND WINNING STREAK

A picture of the Tech varsity was smack in the center of the page and a double-column story followed. Chip glanced at the picture, struck once more by the team's lack of height. "The biggest one isn't much taller than I am," he marveled. "Not many teams go undefeated without a couple of big men."

He studied the faces of the Tech stars and was engrossed in his study when Soapy slipped into the seat opposite. One look at Soapy's worried face was enough for Chip. "What's the matter? Are you sick?"

Soapy shook his head. "Not the way you mean, Chip. But I'm sick enough, just the same."

"Why? What happened?"

"Plenty. Parks and Minton came to the store last night just as we were closing up and asked me if I'd mind taking a little ride with them." Soapy sighed. "Well, to make a long story short, I got in their car and drove out to the gas station. As if I didn't know where we were going. And when we got there, they put a hat on my head—it was brown this time. . . .

"Then they gave me a blue sweater and told me to put that on and sit behind the wheel of their car. They took the keys out first, and then they asked me to lean out the window and hand Welsh a dollar bill."

"What happened then?"

"Well, Welsh said—and these are his exact words —'It looks just like him!' he says. 'I told you it was him a week ago!'"

Soapy snorted disgustedly. "How about that?"

"How about that is right! Then what?"

"We drove back to State Drug and went to Mr. Grayson's office. Then they told him about Welsh and asked me about a hundred times the same things they had already asked me a hundred times."

"How long did this go on?"

"Until about midnight."

"Didn't Mr. Grayson say anything?"

"Sure! When Parks told him about Welsh, Mr. Grayson said he wouldn't put any credence whatever in anything Welsh said. Then Parks said Welsh had made a positive identification, and Mr. Grayson said that he wouldn't believe Welsh on a stack of Bibles as high as his desk.

"Then Mr. Grayson said he couldn't see how Welsh's latest identification had changed anything."

"What did Parks and Minton say to that?"

"Well, Minton said that he and Parks were on the spot because Welsh had called the chief of police. That's why they took me out to the station and made me put on the hat and the sweater.

"Then Mr. Grayson said he would call the chief of police the first thing Monday morning, that's to-morrow, and— Well, I guess that's it."

Both boys sat quietly for some time. Then Soapy broke the silence. "Parks and Minton think I'm guilty, Chip. I can tell by the way they act. What am I going to do?"

"Nothing," Chip said shortly. "You are innocent and it's up to them to find the guilty person."

During the long silence which followed, Chip was scribbling on a piece of paper, doodling idly. Then he began to sketch the face of the driver of the car.

Soapy watched him appreciatively. "It's a perfect likeness. Right down to the last detail. The glasses even look the same."

"The glasses!" Chip said excitedly. "That's it! It's the glasses. Where's that paper?" He leafed impatiently through the *Herald*. "Here it is," he breathed.

Chip spread the paper out on the table and made several quick strokes on the page. "It could be."

"Could be what?" Soapy asked.

"Could be we've located your pal," Chip said, shoving the newspaper under Soapy's nose. "Recognize anyone?"

CHAPTER 12

A SHOT IN THE DARK

"It's him!" Soapy cried excitedly. "I'm sure it's him! The glasses make the difference. He's the fellow who changed the tire!"

"Maybe yes, and maybe no," Chip cautioned. "Take it easy, now. Don't jump the gun."

"What's his name?" Jimmy asked.

Chip ran his finger along the names below the picture. "Bill Sanders. He's the captain of the team."

"How about that!" Soapy said. "The captain of the Tech team . . ."

"He'll be easy to find," Jimmy said. "Everybody on the Tech campus will know him."

"That's for sure," Chip said. "I'd better call Mr. Grayson."

"Let me call Mitzi first," Soapy said, rushing for the telephone booth. "I promised her I'd call the first thing if something happened."

Seconds later, Soapy slammed out of the booth. "She's driving down. Right away! Going to drive us out there. Boy, was she ever happy!"

"Don't count on it too much, Soapy," Chip warned. "It's just a shot in the dark."

"Uh, uh," Soapy said confidently. "It's him. It's gotta be him."

Chip called Mr. Grayson and told him about the picture and added that Mitzi was driving them out to the Tech campus.

"Fine, Chip," George Grayson said happily. "Be sure to let me know how you make out. Mrs. Grayson and I will be home all evening."

When Chip finished the call, Soapy and Jimmy were at the counter comparing the sketch with the news picture. "What a break," Jimmy said.

Soapy was on top of the world. "What do you mean break?" he demanded. "It wasn't a break! Chip did it scien— Oh, heck . . . efficiently."

"Well, scientifically or efficiently," Jimmy retorted, "Pete and I will be waiting right here until you get back. Remember, now, we'll be here if we have to stay open all night."

Several blasts of a car horn in front of the restaurant sent Soapy scurrying to the door. "C'mon, Chipper, it's Mitzi. See you later, Jimmy. We'll bring 'em back dead or alive!"

Tech was located in a small village five miles east of University. Mitzi covered the distance speedily and slowed the car down when the first "Twenty-five miles per hour" sign appeared. "Now what?" she asked.

"We take a tour," Soapy said quickly. "The drugstore first, naturally. If we have no luck there, we hit a frat or a sorority, and, er—"

"Then we'll go to the dean's home," Chip added.

They found the drugstore, easily enough, right on a corner. And it was open. "Bill Sanders?" the soda clerk repeated. "Sure, I know him. Greatest basketball player in Tech history."

"Where can we find him?" Chip asked.

"Not right now. The team played in Chicago last night. Won again, too! Thirteen straight now. I don't think they're back yet."

"Do you know his telephone number?"

"I can get it. Just a sec." The clerk consulted a telephone book and wrote the number down. Chip then tried calling, but there was no answer.

Back in the car, they paused to talk it over. Mitzi came up with the best suggestion. "Let's call Mr. Grayson. He'll know what to do."

"Good idea," Chip agreed. "We'll call from Pete's Place."

Back at University they stopped in front of the restaurant. Jimmy and Pete rushed out to the car. "Any luck?" Jimmy asked.

"No," Chip explained. "The team isn't in town."

Chip then called the Grayson residence. His friendly employer suggested that they drive out to his home. "Bring Pete and Jimmy with you," he said.

Pete and Jimmy were enthusiastic when Chip told them of the invitation. "Let's go!" Pete said jubilantly. "I wouldn't miss any part of this if you *gave* me George Grayson's drugstore."

George Grayson was one of University's wealthiest and most influential citizens. But it wasn't reflected in his mode of living and humble manner. Mrs. Grayson was the same type of person, sweet, unaffected, and friendly. They listened quietly while Chip related the events of the evening.

Later, while Mrs. Grayson was serving refreshments, the genial host excused himself. Returning in a few minutes, he said, "I just talked to Dean Engle at Tech. He promised to have Bill Sanders in my office tomorrow morning at ten o'clock. Can you make it, Soapy?"

"Yes, *sir!* I sure can!"

"I'll be there too," Chip said firmly.

Chip didn't get much rest that night. Neither did Soapy. Each tried to conceal his restlessness from the other, breathing evenly, simulating sleep although both were wide awake. Soapy was the first to break. "All right!" he exploded abruptly, sitting up in bed and pulling on his desk light. "Let's cut out the faking. So we can't sleep!"

"Right!" Chip agreed. "Let's take a walk."

George Grayson's office was overcrowded this particular morning. Mr. Grayson sat behind his desk and Parks and Minton sat with their backs to the picture window facing the front of the store. Chip and Soapy sat directly opposite the two detectives. The atmosphere was heavy and uneasy and ominously quiet, despite the steady clatter of Ann Tracy's typewriter in the outer office.

Chip was extremely uncomfortable and wished someone would break the silence. Then the outside office door opened and he heard Ann Tracy say:

"Yes, he's expecting you. Go right in."

Scarcely able to stand the suspense, Chip glanced at his pal. Soapy was leaning forward, his legs bunched under his chair, every muscle in his body tense and ready. Then he leaped to his feet and rushed toward the broad-shouldered athlete who was framed momentarily in the door.

"Oh, boy!" Soapy cried exultantly. "Am I glad to see you! Remember me?"

Soapy almost lifted the newcomer from the floor

as he pulled him forward. Recognition dawned suddenly in Bill Sanders' eyes. "Hey!" he said, peering at Soapy through his glasses. "Sure! I remember you. You're the guy with the flat tire!"

There was no question about the recognition. Sanders shook hands with Soapy and then the redhead introduced Chip and Mr. Grayson and Gil Minton and Fred Parks. Sanders was obviously in the dark and, after the introductions, looked inquiringly at Soapy. "What's this all about? Dean Engle excused me from my classes and said—"

"Excuse me, Sanders, Soapy," Grayson said quickly. "Perhaps Mr. Parks and Mr. Minton can handle this better than anyone else."

Detective Parks took it from there, avoiding all reference to the robbery but making it clear that any information Bill Sanders could provide concerning the date, time, and place of the tire incident was of extreme importance to Soapy.

Sanders answered Parks' questions quickly and surely, and Gil Minton quietly entered each response in the familiar notebook. The date was unequivocally verified. Tech had played a home basketball game that Wednesday night, and Sanders and his two teammates, Stew Wilson and Ed Henry, were on their way to University for something to eat when they saw Smith in the road.

Sure, he remembered the spot, all right. He had made the drive between University and the Tech campus many times during his three and a half years in school. The time was somewhere between eleven thirty and eleven forty-five because he and his two pals were in the Central Restaurant in University five minutes before closing time at midnight.

Then Minton took charge, and Parks jotted down

the notes. Sanders told Minton that the basketball game was over at approximately ten thirty because his teammates remarked about the long game and noted the time while they were dressing.

He and his two teammates drove to their boarding-house just off the campus. But they were in no mood to go to bed, and since training rules were canceled after game nights, they decided to drive to University.

Sanders was sure and precise with his answers. Detective Minton finished his questioning, at last, and glanced ruefully at Parks. "I guess that's it, Fred," he said, spreading his hands in a gesture of resignation. "What do you think?"

Parks shook his head slowly, whistling softly as he looked frcm Sanders to Soapy. He shrugged his shoulders and rose slowly to his feet. "Thanks, Sanders," he said, nodding to the tall athlete, "you've been a big help. Do you suppose we could locate Henry and Wilson without too much difficulty?"

"Sure. You'll find them at the Tech drugstore at twelve o'clock. Right on the dot. We meet there every day for lunch."

"Thanks. We'll drive over. Right now! Come on, Gil." At the door Parks paused. "Oh, yes. I'll call you at two o'clock, Mr. Grayson."

"I'll be here," Grayson replied shortly. "Two o'clock sharp." He turned to Sanders. "How about being my guest for lunch?"

"Excuse me, sir," Chip interrupted. "Pete is expecting Soapy and me for lunch. Bill might like to go along with us."

Grayson nodded. "I think that would be nice. Oh, by the way, Chip, I wish you would drop back here at two o'clock."

Lunch was waiting at the restaurant and Jimmy and the jovial owner were eager to hear the details. Chip brought Bill Sanders up to date.

"That was some experience," Sanders said, shaking his head ruefully. "I wouldn't want to have those two men on my trail."

Chip left Soapy, Sanders, Jimmy and Pete shortly before two o'clock and hustled back to Mr. Grayson's office. His employer was on the telephone and gestured toward a chair when Chip entered.

It was the first time Chip had ever seen George Grayson angry. His employer's face was red, and his lips were pressed into a thin, determined line. He suddenly banged a fist on his desk making the pen-and-ink set jump. "This has gone far enough! By your own admission, Parks, the Tech boys verified Smith's story. What's this *new* nonsense?"

George Grayson grew more perturbed with each word he heard. "That's enough, Parks," he said sharply. "Why didn't you tell me about it this morning?" He listened intently, nervously tapping the desk with his fingers. "Nonsense! This is ridiculous."

He moved the telephone base roughly to the side of his desk and jammed the receiver down on the cradle. Then he leaned back in his chair and shook his head disgustedly. "You'll never believe this, Chip. Parks now says the robbery could have taken place as much as twenty minutes earlier. The service-station clock gains that much every twelve hours. George Ringo—he's the owner—sets the clock himself each morning and the station crew set it back from time to time during the day when they notice the discrepancy. They don't remember turning it back the day of the robbery. . . ."

CHAPTER 13

A NEW FRIENDSHIP

BILL SANDERS was laughing heartily when Chip glanced through the window of Pete's restaurant. Soapy was back in stride and his audience was enjoying him. Badly as he felt, Chip had to grin as he watched his pal's facial distortions and expansive gestures. Then he remembered the bad news he carried and his face sobered.

The levity ceased when Chip opened the door. "It's about time," Pete said. "What's the good word?"

"It isn't," Chip said grimly. Then he told them about the gas-station clock and the failure of the crew to turn it back.

"How can they be sure they didn't?" Pete demanded. "Some memory!"

"That puts us right back where we started," Soapy said soberly.

"Maybe," Chip said. "Anyway, I've got to get started. I've got to see Murph Kelly and I'm late."

"Me, too," Sanders said. "I've got a mid-term first thing in the morning. Come on. I'll drop you and Jimmy off at the field house. It's right on my way."

Chip, Jimmy, and Bill got better acquainted on

the short drive to the field house, and when they parted, the three boys had formed a new friendship.

"See you soon," Sanders called cheerily when they parted. "Happy hunting."

Murph Kelly was all alone when the two boys reached the dressing room. He greeted Chip sourly. "You shouldn't be here. After your treatment, beat it! And don't come back until Wednesday. I hope you're not figuring on playing against Western."

"I'm going to play if Doc will let me."

"We'll cross that bridge when we come to it," Kelly retorted.

Chip devoted the following day to his new plans. And that night all of Soapy's friends were on hand. He had prepared a new watch list, and, encouraged by the success achieved through the sketch of Bill Sanders, Chip had made a drawing of the man Welsh had described, using Soapy as a model. A long discussion followed. Just before the meeting broke up, Chip gave them the revised watch list.

Dr. Terring put Chip through a long examination Wednesday afternoon and gave him permission to play. "Providing," he said pointedly, "you remember your word-of-honor promise."

Coach Corrigan used Chip sparingly in the game, playing him only a minute or two at a time. Nevertheless, he managed to get fourteen points and the Statesmen squeezed through another toughie. The score: State 73, Western 71.

Chip's leg was so stiff after he finished his shower that he could scarcely make it up the steps to the street. He was glad to see Mitzi's car waiting at the usual place with Soapy at the wheel.

The next morning, every step was an effort, and he had a difficult time walking from one classroom to the next. Later, when he hobbled into the training room, Kelly hit the ceiling. "I knew it! Now you sit right where you are until I get back."

The trainer stormed out of the room, slamming the door behind him. In a few minutes he was back with Coach Corrigan and Dr. Terring. "See for yourself," he said testily. "It's swollen up again. You'd better lay him off for a good rest. If you don't, he isn't going to be worth a dime when you need him most—against Brandon and A. & M."

"Right!" Coach Corrigan said decisively.

Dr. Terring gave the knee a thorough examination and then took a basketball schedule out of his pocket. He studied it thoughtfully, pulling at his chin and mumbling under his breath. "Let's see. You play Midwestern here Saturday night, and Cathedral and Wesleyan away on the eleventh and twelfth. The next game is with Brandon on February nineteenth. Hmm . . .

"This is the third. I'd say he should have two weeks' rest—"

"Wait a second!" Chip interrupted. "Nothing doing! No, sir! Why, the season will be practically over—"

"Be quiet, Chip," Kelly said.

Dr. Terring continued thoughtfully, "That will bring him up to the seventeenth, and he will probably be ready to play against Brandon on the nineteenth."

"Good!" Kelly cried. "How about the treatments?"

"We'll skip everything for a week," Terring said decisively. "Give the knee a complete rest." He turned to Chip. "Now I don't want you to do any practicing or running or anything else until February seventeenth. That's an order."

The days passed quickly. It was a relief to have nothing to do in the afternoons except study. But, as the days passed and nothing happened on the night watches, Chip began to think that his plans were a little on the foolish side. But he wasn't going to quit.

Jim Locke took a few pot shots at Chip in the *News* but Soapy's trouble had taken the edge off of the sports writer's sarcastic quips. Chip scarcely gave them a thought. Saturday night he sat on the bench and watched State slip past Midwestern in the last twenty seconds to win another close game, 67 to 66.

Sunday, back in his room after church, Chip settled himself comfortably in his study chair and read the papers. Soapy had gone out on an errand, but he had opened the *News* to the sports pages, and Jim Locke's column was again marked in red. Chip anticipated something personal but he was wholly unprepared for the shocker he found in the second paragraph.

Chip Hilton, the defending champion, Sky Bollinger, the runner-up, and Bitsy Reardon, another strong contender, are local entries in the National Marksmanship Tournament, scheduled for next Friday and Saturday, February 11 and 12.

Hilton's ailing knee has conveniently placed him on the "ex-athletics" list, and he will undoubtedly be present for the opening ceremonies. It will be interesting to see what Bollinger and Reardon will do to insure their participation in the tournament while the State basketball team is on the road . . .

Chip read the paragraph several times, mulling it over in his mind. Then he picked up the *Herald*.

Bill Bell presented a picture of the conference situation in his column and drew attention to the race between Western, A. & M., and Brandon for leadership. He advanced the opinion that the winner would probably be in line for the district N.C.A.A. representation.

Chip studied the standing of the teams. State was in fourth place and likely to stay there.

CONFERENCE STANDINGS

Teams	Won	Lost
Brandon	18	3
A. & M.	15	3
Western	14	3
State	17	6

The Tech record of fifteen victories and no defeats was featured in a separate paragraph, and Bell gave the Engineers an outside chance for district representation should the conference contenders weaken in their down-the-stretch drive.

The second sports page of the *Herald* was devoted to the Marksmanship Tournament. Entry lists and photographs of the leading contenders in the state and national picture filled the page. Chip's picture was featured in the center of the page. He laid the *Herald* aside and reread the second paragraph of Locke's column in the *News*.

"Soapy is right," he murmured. "Locke never gives up."

Chip remained close to Jeff the rest of the day, hitting the books and trying to keep Jim Locke out of his thoughts. Soapy joined him later, aware of Chip's feelings but thoughtfully silent, and the two pals spent the evening in study. Just before going to bed, they took a long walk and then returned to Jeff and went to bed. But not to sleep. Soapy was conjuring up a dream in which Jim Locke struggled in the middle of a big lake filled with black ink, struggling vainly like a fly caught on a piece of sticky flypaper.

"Now stew in your own juice," Soapy muttered.

"What?"

"Nothing, Chip. I was just daydreaming."

Chip tossed fitfully all night. But when he got up Monday morning he had reached an important decision. He was going to see Bill Bell and drop out of the tournament.

Bill Bell had just finished his work when Chip arrived at the sports editor's desk. He greeted Chip with a smile and waved to the chair beside his desk. "Sit down, Chip. How are you? What brings you around here?"

Chip took a deep breath. "I want to drop out of the tournament."

"Drop out?"

"Yes, sir. It isn't fair to the team."

Bill Bell pushed his chair back from the desk and leaned forward to face Chip. "I don't understand. Why isn't it fair to the team?"

"A lot of people think I am using my knee as an alibi, so I can practice my shooting."

"A lot of people! Nonsense! Every intelligent person in this town knows that Doc Terring decides when a player is able to play."

Chip nodded uncertainly. "But Sky Bollinger and Bitsy Reardon told me *they* were going to drop out."

"There's a little difference, Chip. In the first place, you're the defending champion and you have a bye until the fourth of March. Bollinger and Reardon are not eligible for byes, as you know. They have to qualify in the state. And, naturally, since those trials fall on the dates of the team's road games, they have no alternative.

"You're in a different position. You don't have to compete in the state. It doesn't make any difference, so far as your position in the tournament is concerned, whether you make the trip or not." Bell paused and eyed Chip patiently. "You understand that, don't you, Chip?"

Chip nodded. "Yes, sir, but not many people know that."

"They will," Bell said grimly. "Now, Chip," he continued understandingly, "I know exactly how Jim Locke's sniping has affected you. I imagine you are familiar with the old saying: 'Sticks and stones may break my bones but names will never hurt me.'" Bell smiled and eyed Chip quizzically. Then he continued significantly, "Doesn't that apply to Jim Locke and the exaggerated opinions he prints in his column?"

"I guess so."

"All through life, Chip, a fellow is faced with situations which provide the opportunity of choosing the hard way or the easy. Right now, your road is a little rough. But I'm betting on you. And I seldom make a mistake when my estimate is based on character. . . .

"Oh, yes. One more thing. A fighter never quits and a quitter never wins. Think it over!"

CHAPTER 14

THE DEAN'S LIST

BILL BELL picked up the telephone as soon as Chip left and called Henry Rockwell at the State Athletic Office. The conversation was brief enough but it accomplished its purpose. At any rate, Bell was smiling when he cradled the receiver. That night Chip was surprised and happy when his old high-school coach walked into State Drug's stockroom.

"Hello, Chip," Rockwell said, sitting down at the desk. "Are you busy?"

"No, Coach. Not at all."

"Good. I thought I'd drop in and say hello. By the way, you seem to make Jim Locke's column about every day. He must be a friend of yours."

Chip grinned. "I don't think so," he said lightly.

Rockwell changed the subject. "What's wrong with Soapy, Chip? Is he in some sort of trouble?"

Chip told Rockwell about Soapy's problem and the steps he and the rest of Soapy's pals were taking to clear up the difficulty.

"I knew there was something wrong. Is there anything I can do?"

"I don't think so, Coach. Not right now, anyway."

"Well, you know where to reach me. I'm sure it will work out all right." Rockwell hesitated, studied Chip searchingly for a second, and then continued gently, "By the way, I hope you're not letting Jim Locke get under your skin."

Chip shook his head. "It doesn't mean a thing, Coach."

"Good! I knew you were too smart to let that bother you. Oh, yes, I'm glad to see you're taking care of that knee. And that reminds me. I talked to Doc Jones on the telephone this morning. He told me everyone down home was pulling for you to hold your shooting championship. I told him that went for Coach Corrigan, the team, and me, too. Well, I guess I'll be getting along."

Later that night, when Chip and Soapy arrived at Pete's Place, Jimmy Lu Chung greeted them with a long face. "Tech got beat tonight," he announced glumly. "Eighty-one to eighty."

"Got it on the radio," Pete added. "Announcer said it was a rough game. Said there was some kind of a rhubarb but didn't give any details. I guess we'll hear about it tomorrow night. Sanders said they would be over about ten o'clock."

"Do you think this will hurt their chances for the N.C.A.A.?" Jimmy asked.

"It shouldn't," Fireball said. "The game was played on the Brandon court and that was a ten-point advantage. A one-point defeat is nothing to be ashamed of against a team like Brandon. Right, Chip?"

"Right. Gosh, I'll bet Bill Sanders is feeling low right now. I don't feel too good myself."

"Well," Soapy said, summing it up, "there's one

thing for sure. Jim Locke can't blame Chip for the defeat. C'mon. Let's go home."

The Thursday issue of the *Herald* played up the tournament, displaying pictures of the contestants and personal stories of their accomplishments. Bill Bell ran a head shot of Chip in his column and devoted the first paragraph to a description of the knee injury. Then he explained that Dr. Mike Terring had side-lined Chip for ten days and that the marksmanship champion would not accompany the team on the road trip.

Bell deplored Tech's first defeat but asserted that the Engineers had lost little stature in the one-point defeat. He pointed out that few teams ever went through a season undefeated.

In the last paragraph, Bell cast the Statesmen in the role of spoilers, citing the importance of the Brandon game away on February 19, the home game on March 2, and the final game of the season against A. & M. on March 7 at Alumni Gym. Victories in these three games, Bell opined, might knock both teams out of the race for the conference honors and push Tech right into the tournament as the sectional representative.

Both Chip and Soapy were tired when they dropped into Pete's Place that night. But they forgot their own troubles when they saw Bill Sanders and his two pals, Stew Wilson and Ed Henry. Sanders was talking heatedly to Pete and Jimmy and waited for Chip and Soapy to get settled. Then he banged the table and continued. "Sure!" he said. "That's exactly the way they play. And they get away with it."

"They sure do!" Stew Wilson said vehemently. "You'll find out, all right. They send one of their

three big men into the pivot in rotation and each
one of them uses the same technique." He leaped
to his feet to demonstrate the play.

"Look!" Stew said, leaning back against Chip and
forcing him against the side of the booth. "You
see what I mean?"

Chip grinned. "I see, all right."

Then Ed Henry got into the act, replacing Wilson. He put all his weight against Chip and held
his position. Then he pretended to catch a ball.
"Now, watch! Watch my elbow!" He raised his left
elbow until it was level with Chip's eyes and turned,
banging it up against Chip's face. Then he emulated
a shot at the basket with his right hand. "Nice trick,
huh?"

"Don't see how they can get away with that,"
Soapy said.

Stew Wilson pushed Ed Henry away. "That's nothing!" he said. "How about this?"

"Hold it!" Chip protested. "I believe you. Honest!"

"That's only a sample, Chip," Sanders said. "They
fouled when they backed into us, all right, but the
real business was the bang in the face."

"They never missed the shot, either," Stew added
dourly. "It was a perfect one-two."

"Then the official would call a foul on one of us,"
Ed Henry said.

"Yeah," Sanders added dryly. "For being stupid
enough to stand still and get hit. Wonderful!"

"Don't worry," Stew Wilson said quietly. "We'll
take care of *them*. This Saturday. They won't pull
that stuff on the officials we have around here."

"Right!" Henry added bitterly. "Our officials call
the games according to the rules."

"I can't wait," Wilson said quietly. "If ever I wanted to beat a team—"

"Don't get us wrong, fellows," Sanders interrupted. "We're not sore because they broke our winning streak. That hurt, all right, but losing is only a small part of it. The real beef, so far as we're concerned, is that they didn't win fairly. That's why we're sore."

"We wouldn't tell this to anyone at Tech," Ed Henry said. "It's not an alibi. We're telling you because we know you won't repeat it."

"That's right," Sanders added, his face lighting up with a grin. "I guess we're just trying to get it out of our systems."

"That's what friends are for," Chip said. "We'll sure be pulling for you Saturday night."

Chip was wrong about that. All the rooting in the world wouldn't have helped Tech Saturday night because Brandon canceled the game. The Brandon Athletic Council had canceled the game scheduled to be played on the Tech court because of the intense feeling which had been evidenced between the players of both teams during and immediately following the game at Brandon.

So Chip's three Tech friends were with him Friday and Saturday nights when the sectional contenders competed for marksmanship positions. Sanders, Wilson, and Henry were upset, bitter because of Brandon's cancellation, but they didn't say much about it. Chip was quiet, too, annoyed by the attention given him by the reporters and photographers. But they were all cheered by the announcement that State had defeated Cathedral 80 to 79 Friday night, and Wesleyan by a score of 63 to 61 Saturday afternoon.

Soapy was propped up in bed, trying to study, when Chip reached Jeff. The redhead closed the book disgustedly and tossed it on the floor. But he grinned cheerfully, trying to cover up the tired and worried lines of his face. "Just can't concentrate, Chip," he said wryly.

Chip couldn't concentrate, either. And that was serious. A fellow who was working his way through school couldn't afford to let anything upset his study program.

The next morning Soapy got the Sunday papers. But when he opened the *News* to the sports pages and started to read Jim Locke's column, Chip checked him.

"Hold it, Soapy. I want to tell you something."

"What?"

"I'm not going to read anything Locke writes until after the basketball season, and I don't want you to tell me about anything he puts in his column."

"Why?"

"Because I don't want to think about the things he writes. Isn't that sensible? If I don't know what he writes it can't worry me."

Soapy nodded his head slowly. "Sure," he said thoughtfully, "that's a good idea." He tossed the *News* aside and picked up the *Herald*.

"What's in the *Herald*?"

"I thought you weren't going to read the papers?"

"Not the papers—just the *News* and Locke's column."

Soapy grinned. "I just asked, old pal. Well, you hit Bill Bell's column. He says the team will have a week of rest, and by the time State meets Brandon you will be back in playing condition. And listen to this: 'Tech continues as the outstanding candidate to represent this section in the N.C.A.A. championships.' Sounds good, eh?"

"It sure does. If any team ever deserved the honor, it's Tech. I don't think any team made up of students, and I mean *students,* ever made a record like theirs. Besides, they're great fellows."

"And then some," Soapy said admiringly. "Imagine! Every player on the team on the Dean's list. That's really something in an engineering school."

"I'll say," Chip agreed.

The days passed quickly enough. Chip had put Jim Locke out of his mind and concentrated on his books and the night watches. And, with the improvement of his knee, the old basketball urge returned. Wednesday afternoon, the day before he was to report back to practice, Chip showed up at State Drug with his basketball shoes.

"Where do you think you're going?" Mitzi demanded.

"Over to the Y," Chip said calmly. "I'm going to see if my knee is as good as it feels."

Chip had no difficulty getting the use of a ball and permission to practice a few shots. His knee felt fine and he became so absorbed with his practice shots that he failed to observe the spectators who were watching his marksmanship. One such observer stared unbelievingly at Chip, and then, grinning delightedly, hurried away. Jim Locke wanted to see Jim Corrigan before writing his next day's column.

CHAPTER 15

SECRET PRACTICE

MURPH KELLY groaned and jerked his head toward the far end of the court. "Oh, oh!" he groaned. "Here comes trouble, Coach. I guess I'd better find some unfinished business."

Corrigan waited uncomfortably as Jim Locke approached. The young coach exerted every bit of his will power to conceal his dislike for the reporter. He was resignedly prepared for the usual probing, baiting, and caustic questioning.

"Hello, Corrigan," Locke said abruptly. "I thought Hilton was supposed to be resting his leg."

"He is."

"That's what you think!"

"I don't understand—" Corrigan was cautious, slightly puzzled. He knew Locke had something up his sleeve, all right, but he wanted to tread easily.

"He's been practicing for Bill Bell's shooting promotion at the Y."

Corrigan shook his head. "I don't follow you."

"You mean you don't or you won't . . ."

"I mean I don't know what you're talking about," Corrigan said curtly. "If you don't mind, Locke, I've got to get on with practice."

"I don't mind," Locke said slyly. "I just thought you ought to know about your injured star's extra-curricular basketball activities? You see, Doc Terring told me that Hilton was to rest his leg until Thursday, February seventeenth, and—well, that's tomorrow. Right?"

Corrigan nodded. "Yes, that's right."

"Well, then, how come he was practicing at the Y? Did he have your permission?"

"No—no, he didn't."

"What are you going to do about it?"

"I don't expect to do anything about it until I know all the circumstances."

"But isn't it the same as breaking training? And isn't it disloyal to the team to practice secretly for —let's say—Bell's shooting match instead of practicing with the team and trying to win games for State?"

"I can't answer that, Locke," Corrigan said slowly, turning away. "You'll have to excuse me now. I've got work to do."

Just about the time Jim Locke was talking to Coach Corrigan, Chip was finishing his little workout at the Y. He was pleased with the condition of his knee and imbued with a tremendous urge to get back with the team. His good spirits carried over to the next day and right up to the moment he entered the dressing room. Then he got a slight shock. Murph Kelly's reception was on the cool side.

"Coach wants to see you, Hilton," Kelly said dourly. "He's in his office."

Coach Corrigan was sitting at his desk when Chip knocked on the open door. "Come in and sit down, Chip," he said slowly. "How's your knee?"

"It's fine Coach. I sure hope Doc Terring will let

me practice." Chip waited uncertainly, sensing that something was wrong.

"That's what I wanted to talk about. Are you sure you've been following Doc's orders?"

"Why, yes, Coach. Sure."

"Then you haven't been practicing on your own?"

"No, sir. Not a bit except a little shooting at the Y.M.C.A. yesterday afternoon." Chip paused and eyed Corrigan uncertainly. "I didn't do a bit of running, Coach. I took maybe forty or fifty easy shots at the basket, that's all. Was that wrong, sir?"

"I don't exactly know, Chip. Have you seen the *News* today? Jim Locke's column?"

Chip grinned slightly. "No, sir, I haven't been reading Mr. Locke's column for some time."

"That's not a bad idea," Corrigan mused. "Think I'll try it myself." He shoved a newspaper clipping across the desk. "Read that."

STATE STAR HOLDS SECRET PRACTICE

Sports Espionage

Many years ago when this reporter was a freshman in college, rival college athletic departments often boasted an efficient sports espionage system. Various emissaries ventured forth in appropriate disguises to seek out the top-drawer secrets of the respective rivals. This development led to counter-espionage practices, such as the posting of security guards and secret team workouts behind closed gates and doors.

Ethics

Inevitably, however, a code of ethics did away with the spying techniques and today rival spies (scouts) are welcomed at various games and given choice seats from which to secure their information.

The above was brought to mind yesterday afternoon when this reporter learned of an unusual type of practice session at the University Y.M.C.A.

SIDE-LINED STAR

Local basketball fans are aware that Chip Hilton, State's high-scoring basketball star, has been side-lined by orders of Dr. Mike Terring for the past few games. Dr. Terring excused Hilton from team practices with specific orders to rest his knee until a thorough examination could be given to the important limb. *That examination is scheduled for this afternoon.*

SECRET PRACTICE

However, this column received an eyewitness report that Hilton has been practicing his National Marksmanship Championship *shots* in secret practices at the local Y.M.C.A.

LOYALTY

Inasmuch as Hilton is a vital member of the State team which has been battling desperately and vainly for a position in the all-important conference standings, the information came as a shock to this columnist. We have always believed that team sports are justifiable, primarily because of the development of loyalty to team and school.

COACH IN THE DARK

State's hoop coach, Jim Corrigan, was informed of Hilton's secret workouts yesterday afternoon and advised this reporter that Hilton did not have his permission to engage in such practices.

"Gosh, Coach," Chip said lamely, shaking his head, "I never dreamed I was doing anything wrong."

"I know," Corrigan said understandingly. "You're sure you practiced just the one time?"

"Positive, Coach. Gee, I'm sorry. I guess there isn't anything else I *can* say."

Corrigan smiled. "That's all you need to say. Forget it. Now you run along and see Doc Terring. I'll call him on the telephone and explain everything. I'll tell Kelly, too."

Murph Kelly was just hanging up the receiver when Chip reached the locker room. He glanced at Chip and shook his head. "That guy causes more trouble than the mumps," he growled disgustedly. "Locke, I mean," he added belligerently. "C'mon. We gotta see Terring."

Dr. Terring smiled wryly when Kelly and Chip arrived in his office. "Coach just called," he said. "I guess the less said, the better. Now, let's have a look at that knee."

Later, Chip followed Murph Kelly back to the locker room and lost no time in suiting up. "I'm glad Coach wasn't sore, Murph," he said happily.

"No thanks to Jim Locke," Kelly growled.

When Chip reached the court, practice was under way. But that meant nothing to the Statesmen when they saw Chip. They stopped right in the middle of one of Corrigan's drills and surrounded him, their enthusiasm fullheartedly and joyously expressed.

"How do you feel, Chipper? Now you take it easy."

"Hope you haven't been paying any attention to those stories in the *News*."

"Say that again! Who does he think he's kidding?"

"Right! Wonder what makes him think we don't want you to win the marksmanship tournament?"

"You gotta win it now. Just to show him up."

"Forget Locke. Bill Bell's a better writer, anyway."

"Who said Locke could write?"

Coach Corrigan's whistle broke up the discussion and Chip and Murph Kelly walked down to the practice basket to limber up. The trainer worked Chip for half an hour, his keen eyes studying every move, and then dismissed him for practice.

"See you tomorrow afternoon, Chip. Now get out of here and take care of that knee."

Chip worked out again Friday afternoon, and when the State basketball squad assembled at University depot that night for the trip to Brandon, he was on hand. Soapy, Bill Sanders, Stew Wilson, and Ed Henry were with him, and Chip introduced the Tech stars to his teammates.

"I think you can take them," Sanders told his new State friends, "but you'll have to stop their big men under the boards. They're plenty tough."

Coach Jim Corrigan had been a quiet listener. Now he entered the conversation. "How do you think a collapsing zone would work?" he asked.

"Good!" Sanders said enthusiastically. "You've got the height and the weight to give them a battle under the boards. We just don't have any really big men. That's why we didn't try it."

"We've got them and we'll try it," Corrigan said grimly. "Thanks for your help, Sanders."

Coach Corrigan followed Sanders' advice the following night and used a two-three zone and floated all five defensive players back under the basket to counter Brandon's oversized forward line. And it worked. Brandon's board attack was held in check, and that equalized control of the ball.

It was a tight, bitter contest. Brandon was up for the game, grimly determined to win, fighting for the conference championship. Perhaps State's aggressive under-the-boards game rattled the Brands. At any rate, the lead changed hands twenty-seven times during the forty minutes of play. Coach Corrigan kept Chip on the bench until the last three minutes of the game. Then, with a minute to play and Brandon leading, 77 to 75, it was a set shot by Chip which enabled State to tie the score.

Brandon held the ball for one shot and took it with ten seconds left. But it spun around the rim and out and Sky Bollinger's elbows were right on the hoop when he took the rebound. He turned in the air and fired the ball three-quarters of the way upcourt to Speed Morris. Speed pegged the ball to Jimmy Lu Chung. Jimmy could have taken the shot, but he turned in the air and whipped the ball back to Chip near the center of the court.

Chip barely had time to aim the ball and let it fly. As it left his hands, the gun ended the game. But it couldn't stop the ball as it arched gracefully and swished through the rim and the net to win the game for State by a score of 79 to 77.

The Statesmen were almost delirious with joy, went after Chip, and tried to get him up on their shoulders. "Yea, Chip! What a shot!"

"Come on, fellows," Chip pleaded. "Cut it out. It was a lucky heave."

But they wouldn't let him go. Chip pulled and twisted away and then he felt the pain. It streaked up his leg like a flash of lightning. Murph Kelly was trying to fight his way to Chip's side, but he was too late. So, when the Statesmen boarded the train that night, Chip was limping badly. But he joined in the happy chattering of his teammates.

"That makes it twenty and six, gang," Markley cried. "We've still got a chance."

"Yea, Chip! What a shot!"

"Gotta take all of them," Randall warned.

"We'll take 'em," Gowdy said confidently. "Chip's back and that's all we need."

Soapy and the Tech crowd met the train when it pulled into University Sunday morning. Sanders and Wilson and Henry shook hands delightedly with every player on the squad. "Boy, what a victory!" Sanders cried. "You sure squared it for us."

"We owe you a vote of thanks, Sanders," Coach Corrigan said gratefully. "Maybe we can do it again on March second. We'll sure try."

Soapy had a taxi waiting for Chip and Speed and on the way to Jeff had to be told all about the great win. Speed obliged and Chip dozed, pleasantly relaxed, forgetting his knee. He was half asleep when the taxi pulled up in front of Jeff. He got out and followed his pals up the walk, determined to go to bed as soon as he reached his room.

But Chip came to life with a start when he reached the first-floor hallway. Detectives Gil Minton and Fred Parks were waiting just inside the door.

Chip dropped his bag. "Now what?"

"Just waiting for Smith, that's all, Hilton," Minton answered quietly.

"Is there something new?" Chip asked, now fully aware of the implications in the detectives' presence at Jeff so early on a Sunday morning.

"We think so," Parks said significantly. "Anyway, another gas station was held up last night . . ."

"By a redheaded fellow about Smith's size," Minton added.

CHAPTER 16

THE TEST OF A MAN

"HERE we go again," Soapy groaned, looking help-lessly at Chip. "This is getting monotonous."

"We don't think it's the most exciting case in history," Parks said dryly. "Where can we talk?"

"We can go in the library," Chip said. "There's no one there at this hour in the morning."

"I think I'll go on upstairs, Chip," Speed said, picking up the bags. "Want me to do anything?"

"I don't think so, Speed. I'll see you a little later."

Jeff's library, really a study room, consisted of a dozen tables and approximately fifty chairs. Chip led the way to a table in a corner of the room. "You don't mind if I stay, do you?"

"I guess not," Parks said. He tossed his notebook across the table to Minton. "You jot down the notes, Gil, and I'll ask the questions."

Minton dated a page. "All set, Fred."

Parks faced Soapy. "Now, Smith, where were you last night about eleven thirty?"

"Why—why I was watching the Triangle Service

Station. Jimmy Lu Chung made the trip with the team and I took his place." Soapy hesitated and then continued uncertainly, "Chip and I and some other fellows have been trying to—"

"To play cops-and-robbers," Parks said impatiently. "Go on."

"Well, that's all."

"What time did you reach this watching place?"

"It was exactly eleven o'clock."

"Was anyone with you?"

"No, sir."

"How do you know it was eleven o'clock?"

"Well, I left Pete's Place at ten forty-five and the Triangle clock showed eleven o'clock when I reached the gate across the street. And it showed twelve o'clock when Welsh closed up."

"Do you know where the City Service Station is?"

"Sure. I go past it two or three times every day."

"How long do you think it takes to walk from the City station to the Triangle station?"

Soapy shook his head. "I don't know, Mr. Parks. I haven't any idea."

"Did anyone see you on watch?"

"I don't think so."

"Then all we have is your word that you were across from the Triangle Service Station from eleven o'clock until Welsh closed at twelve. Right?"

"I guess so."

"All right, Smith," Parks said, rising to his feet, "suppose we ride down to the City Service Station and talk to the fellow who was on duty last night. We asked him to meet us there this morning."

Chip had never felt so helpless in his life. There hadn't been a thing he could say or do to help Soapy.

All he could do right now was stick with Soapy and see it through. "Do you mind if I go along, Mr. Parks?" he asked.

Parks glanced at Minton. "How about it, Gil?"

Minton pondered a brief second and then shook his head. "I don't think so, Fred. It's just a matter of identification. Smith will be right back if he's in the clear. Otherwise, we can call Hilton."

"I'll be right here," Chip said grimly, turning to Soapy. "Don't worry."

Soapy nodded and forced a grin. "Imagine! Another guy with freckles and red hair who looks like me! Unbelievable, Dr. Watson. Unbelievable! Well, let's go."

It was a long hour. Speed, Biggie, and Red Schwartz joined Chip in his room and they waited impatiently. Speed was striding restlessly back and forth, pausing each time at the window to look down on the street. "Suppose this guy identifies Soapy," he said worriedly.

"He won't," Chip said confidently. "It just isn't possible."

"It was possible with Welsh," Red said quickly.

"There couldn't be another like Welsh," Chip said.

"One thing is for sure," Biggie said. "There's a guy somewhere in this town who looks like Soapy. And I mean really looks like him."

"Unless he wears a wig," Chip said, grinning. "Hey," he continued thoughtfully, "maybe he does! It sounds silly, I know, but there's got to be some reason no one has seen the fellow."

"Here they are!" Speed said excitedly. "Soapy's getting out of the car. Alone! And Parks and Minton are driving away."

Chip was the first one out of the room but he didn't

have much of a lead. They met Soapy just as he opened the street door and overwhelmed him with questions. "What happened?" "Is everything all right?" "What did he say?" "Did he identify you?"

"Hey! One at a time," Soapy cried. "Anyway, there wasn't much to it. The guy said the holdup fellow was about my size and had red hair, all right, but he didn't think I was the man. Boy, did Parks and Minton take *that* hard! They asked him a lot of questions but they couldn't get anything else out of him. What a life!"

Dr. Mike Terring was obdurate. "No, sir! You're not practicing and you're not playing. You're going to rest that knee—for a week."

"But, Doc, we've still got a chance for the conference title."

Terring grinned. "With a twenty and six record? Not a chance."

"But if we win all the rest, Doc, we'll end up with a twenty-four and six record. That's an eighty-per-cent average. We can *win!*"

"Sure!" Kelly said scathingly. "Sure we can! All we have to do is ask A. & M., Brandon, and Western to lay down and play dead. Nothing to it!"

"It's possible, Murph," Dr. Terring said.

"I've got to play," Chip said. "We've got to beat A. & M. and Brandon."

"Yeah," Kelly said. "It's a matter of life or death."

"It means a lot to me," Chip said.

"I know, Chip," Dr. Terring said kindly. "I'm sorry, but I'll have to order you to stop all basketball activity for a week. Until next Monday. Then we'll talk about Brandon and A. & M."

It was a tough blow. Chip took Dr. Terring's orders literally and didn't even watch the practices. He went directly to work after his classes and took his turn on the night watches. About the only ray of sunshine was the regular and loyal reporting of Soapy's pals. Friday and Saturday brought the final and disastrous blow to State's conference championship hopes. Carlton defeated the Statesmen 56 to 54 on Friday night, and Riordon topped them 51 to 49 on Saturday night. Pete was talking to the Tech crowd when Chip and Soapy arrived.

"Hiya, Chip, Soapy," Pete said glumly. "I guess we can hang up our shoes now. Right?"

"Not yet!" Chip said.

Pete shrugged. "Don't get it. What's left?"

"Brandon and A. & M.," Soapy said. "Beating A. & M. is as good as winning the championship."

"And are we pulling for you to beat Brandon again!" Bill Sanders said fervently.

"We'll kill 'em!" Soapy growled. "Chip will be back Monday."

"To see Doc Terring," Chip corrected.

"You'll play," Soapy said confidently.

Stew Wilson thumped his fist on the table. "You can knock 'em both out of the championship. Brandon *and* A. & M.!"

"Don't forget Western," Sanders reminded him. "A. & M., Brandon, and Western all have identical records. Twenty and four with one game left to play. If State can beat Brandon and A. & M., and Western loses to Southern, it will throw the conference into a three-way tie."

"And put Tech in the national championships," Soapy added. "*That*, my dear pals, would make *everybody* in this town happy."

"It's too much to ask for," Sanders said lightly.

"Come on. I'm going home. I'll drop you fellows off at the dorm."

On the short drive to Jeff, Sanders, Henry, and Wilson talked excitedly about State's coming games with Brandon and A. & M. "Aw, we're dreaming," Ed Henry said. "We wouldn't get the bid if the conference *did* end in a tie."

"Sure you would," Soapy said stoutly. "You're the best team around right now. All you have to do is beat Wilson Tech next Tuesday night."

"They're pretty tough," Sanders replied worriedly.

"You'll take 'em," Soapy said. "Shucks, Chip got fifty-five points against them."

"Fifty-five!" Henry echoed.

"And set a new record," Soapy boasted.

"They went to the semifinals of the Holiday Invitational Tournament, remember," Wilson warned. "And they've already been invited to represent section nine."

"That's the reason you've got to beat them Tuesday night," Soapy concluded. "You beat Wilson Tech and we'll take Brandon and A. & M. That will mean a green light for you to represent this section."

"It's a little too much to hope for," Sanders said wistfully.

Chip was listening intently, watching the faces of his Tech friends. "If only Doc Terring will let me play," he breathed to himself.

The next morning, while Chip was dressing, Soapy read the Sunday papers, commenting as usual on each bit of basketball news. Chip grinned to himself and pretended not to notice when the redhead surreptitiously crammed the *News* into the drawer of his study desk.

"Bill Bell says State is cast in the role of a spoiler,

Chip. He says we can knock them all out of the running."

"All but Western."

"Southern will take them," Soapy predicted. "Hey, where are *you* going?"

"I'm going to church and then I'm going to take a walk. Then I'm going to study all afternoon."

"Me, too. I'll be back after I wash Mitzi's car."

Chip attended church services and then walked slowly down Main Street, stopping from time to time to window-shop. But he noted little of the contents of the windows. His mind was busy with Soapy's problem and the disastrous basketball season. He was startled when someone tapped him on the shoulder. "Thinking about your spring wardrobe?"

Chip pivoted to face Lieutenant Byrnes. "Gosh, no," he said, recovering quickly. "I was thinking about Soapy."

Lieutenant Byrnes nodded. "I can understand that. You know, Chip, Fred and Gil would like to help Smith, and, in my opinion, they will. But you must try to understand their problem. If, as you suggest, the actual thief resembles Smith, Fred and Gil have no other way to strike on the point of resemblance except by talking to Smith and trying to find the key to the matter."

"Does a red wig sound extreme?"

"Nothing is extreme. Now you take it easy and keep me posted on your progress. We'll get a break on this case before you know it."

"Soapy could stand a break," Chip said.

Byrnes shot a quick glance at Chip. Then he grasped Chip's shoulder and gave it a little shake. "A fellow makes his own breaks, Chip. And the real test of a man comes when things look the blackest."

CHAPTER 17

WHAT PRICE GLORY

PETE'S PLACE was deserted. Jimmy Lu Chung was leaning dejectedly on the counter reading the sports page of the *News* when Chip entered. Jimmy hastily closed the paper and tossed it aside. "Hiya, Chip," he said ruefully. "Well, we weren't good enough. If we ever needed you, it was last night and the night before. Carlton and Riordon both played possession ball and beat us at our own game."

"How about the press?"

"We tried it. But you're the only real passer we have. So . . ."

"I sure wish I could have played."

Jimmy hooked a thumb toward the newspaper. "Did you read Locke's column today?"

Chip shook his head. "No. I'm not interested. Well, I guess I'd better get back to Jeff and hit the books. See you tomorrow at practice, I hope."

Soapy had not returned when Chip reached Jeff and he sat down at his desk and tried to study. But it was no go. He couldn't get Jimmy's reference to the story in the *News* out of his mind. Eventually, curiosity got the better of him and he looked for the paper. He found it wadded up and crammed in the wastebasket beside Soapy's desk, but Locke's column had been cut out of the paper.

Chip tried once more to concentrate on his books. But nothing registered. He shut the book, went to Soapy's desk, and pulled open the drawer. There, on top of a pile of similar clippings, was the one he was seeking: Sunday, February 27.

Chip started to close the drawer but the urge was too strong. "If it's going to bother me this much," he muttered, "I might as well read it."

STATE OUT OF CONFERENCE RACE

Feb. 27—All hopes for the miracle which would keep State in the race for conference honors were dissipated by Carlton and Riordon on Friday and Saturday nights. Carlton played possession basketball Friday night to win by a score of 56 to 54, and Riordon followed suit last night to deal the final blow by outlasting State in an uninteresting ball-control game by a score of 51 to 49.

State can now concentrate on Brandon and the "game of the year" against A. & M. Although Brandon is still in the running, A. & M. is a strong favorite to win the loop title and to represent this section in the national (N.C.A.A.) championship tourney.

While his teammates were battling to stay in the conference race, Chip Hilton, State's scoring star, was resting his knee in preparation for the national marksmanship tourney which will be held in Alumni Gym this coming Friday and Saturday.

WHAT PRICE GLORY

This writer has looked in vain for a listing of this shooting contest in State's athletic program. Apparently it outranks every team honor in sight (particularly the State basketball team). . . .

Anger flooded Chip's face as he leafed through the other clippings and a feeling of resentment surged through him until he could scarcely control his emotions. Each of the clippings were written in the same vein.

Feb. 25—Hilton remains behind, presumably to practice for the shooting tourney.

Feb. 20—State ekes out important win with no thanks to the marksmanship champion.

Feb. 19—Hilton has condescended to play tonight.

Feb. 18—Is Coach Corrigan promoting the A.A.U. Marksmanship Championship Tournament or trying to win games for State? This reporter watched Chip Hilton practice "tourney" shots while his teammates worked on team play.

Feb. 17—How long has Chip Hilton's secret shooting practice been going on? Dr. Mike Terring restricted him from *all* athletics because of his temperamental knee.

That ruined the day for Chip. He went for a long walk and brooded. After his return, he fought a losing battle with his books. He just couldn't concentrate. Soapy was in a similar state of mind and the two friends passed a quiet and moody evening.

Chip was in a highly nervous state when he reported for practice Monday afternoon. But he put on a good show for Murph Kelly and Dr. Terring, and the physician gave him permission to shoot around and limber up his knee. Chip dressed slowly and joined his teammates out on the court. They were low, too. But they were glad to see him.

"Sorry we couldn't win, Chip," Markley said, gripping his hand.

"Sorry I couldn't be there to help," Chip said.

"You helped," Thornhill said, putting his arm over Chip's shoulder. "You carried us through a lot of games. It was about time we did something for you."

"That's right," Gowdy said, joining the circle, "and we're sick and tired of Jim Locke and the way he's been riding you. Just to show him up, we're going to take Brandon and A. & M. and put Tech in the N.C.A.A. if it's the last thing we ever do. Just for you. Right, gang?"

The response left no doubt about the feelings of his teammates. Chip couldn't have said anything then to save his life. Fortunately, Coach Corrigan sent him down to the practice basket. "I've got to do my part," Chip was thinking.

Steeling himself to ignore his leg and move freely when he took his shots, Chip forgot all about Jim Locke. Suddenly he felt someone watching him and turned to meet the glance of the one person he least wanted to see.

"How come, Hilton?" Jim Locke asked, grinning. "You too good to practice with the rest of the team?"

Chip's chest contracted. It required an effort to breathe evenly. "Dr. Terring is the boss," he said slowly. "He said I could only shoot around a little."

"You mean practice for Bill Bell's shooting show, don't you?"

Chip shook his head. "No, Mr. Locke, I don't. I've never intentionally practiced for the marksmanship tournament when I worked out with the team."

Locke eyed Chip warily. "I wonder," he said.

Chip bounced the ball on the floor, counting all the while to himself. When he reached ten, he paused. "That's right, Mr. Locke," he said evenly, twirling the ball in his hands. "I never did—

"But I'll tell you this: I like to shoot and this week I intend to practice every chance I get. And what's more, I'm going to try my best to keep the shooting championship."

"I can believe that, all right."

Chip bent over and rolled the ball slowly toward Murph Kelly who was hurrying down the court. Then he straightened up and took a long step toward the columnist. "Now that we understand one another, Mr. Locke," he said, "suppose you leave me alone."

"You can't talk to me like that," Locke cried.

"I think I can," Chip said, advancing toward him.

"Hold it, Chip!" Kelly cried. "Don't do anything foolish." He stepped between the two and faced Locke. "You'd better leave, Mr. Locke. And don't come back until the Coach gives you permission."

Coach Corrigan had approached unheard. "That won't be necessary," he said sharply. "From now on, practices will be closed to everyone." He faced the angry reporter. "And that includes you, Locke. Particularly you. Now, get out!"

Coach Corrigan's barring Jim Locke from practices was second only to the victorious conquest of the Holiday Invitational Tournament in building up the Statesmen's morale. They came to life with a bang, and, taking their cue from Chip, their motto became:

"Put Tech in the national tournament!"

Chip and Soapy went to the Tech–Wilson game Tuesday night and saw Bill Sanders, Ed Henry, Stew Wilson and their teammates bring their wonderful season to an end by defeating Wilson 78 to 70. Afterward, Chip and Soapy escorted their Clinton friend, Greg Moran, captain and Wilson star scoring ace, back to University and to Pete's Place. The victorious Tech gang and practically all of the Valley Falls crowd were on hand.

"Well, you've done your part," Soapy told the Tech stars. "Now, it's up to Chip, Jimmy, and the gang to put you guys in the tournament. And they're going to do it!"

Soapy was right so far as Brandon was concerned. But it wasn't easy. When State and Brandon lined up for the opening tap on Wednesday night, the visitors were up and ready for a fight. State was just as eager, but they were too tight and tried too hard. Both teams held the ball and played cautiously. The Brandon players used their height and bulk to better advantage under the boards this time and slowly forged ahead.

Coach Corrigan kept Chip out of the game until the last ten minutes. Right then, Chip got a lot of practice for the marksmanship tournament. Jimmy, Speed, Sky, and Markwell let him do all the shooting.

Chip had never felt more confident. He took nine shots and every one of them was for his Tech friends. Seven of the nine rippled the cords. Then, with five seconds left to play, he was fouled in the act of shooting and dropped both charity tosses through the hoop to win the game for State, 62 to 61. And that put Brandon out of the running for the conference championship.

Thursday morning, much to Soapy's amazement, it was Chip who brought the *News* and read Locke's column. "Listen to this, Soapy." He laughed. "Locke says I hogged the ball and took all the team's shots.

"And you know something?" he continued. "He hasn't seen anything—yet. I'm going to win the shooting contest and I'm going to shoot every chance I get against A. & M."

Soapy was bewildered. "Are you feeling all right?"

"Sure I'm all right. Now get this! Locke says I'll probably be too exhausted after the Marksmanship Tournament to play in the blood— Oh, boy! To play in the 'blood' game against A. & M." Chip laughed. "He's sure going to be disappointed, Soapy."

"I'll say he is," Soapy said confidently. "This time Saturday night you'll be the winner and still champion. Now, lemme think. What did I say before? I've got it! Wait and see!"

Just about that time, Bill Bell was concentrating on his column. He stressed the Marksmanship Tournament but he didn't forget Tech. He said the Engineers had proved their championship caliber and were entitled to a chance in the National Championship Tournament.

When Bell finished his morning's work, the veteran reporter sighed with satisfaction and leaned back in his chair. Then he saw a copy of the *News* on his desk and opened it to Jim Locke's column. He read the column several times, frowning and shaking his head angrily. "This is *too* much," he growled.

He sat quietly in his chair for a few seconds and then came to a sudden decision. Swinging around to his typewriter he began a letter to Jim Locke. It was a long letter and it contained a lot of strong, straight-from-the-shoulder advice pertaining to the ethical and accurate reporting of news and sports.

Nearly fifty years of experience backed up the philosophies and principles embodied in the contents. Bell grunted approval when he signed the final page. "That ought to do it," he murmured. "If the fellow possesses any decency at all."

CHAPTER 18

CHAMPIONSHIP SPOT

CHIP was embarrassed by all the attention. Flash bulbs were exploding all around him and the reporters were shooting questions at him a mile a minute. Beyond the circle of faces he could see Soapy, Speed, Biggie, Red, Bill Sanders, Stew Wilson, Ed Henry, Fireball, Whitty, and Jimmy Lu Chung. A little way behind them he saw George Grayson, Mrs. Grayson, and Mitzi Savrill. Mitzi waved her handkerchief and Chip waved back.

"How does it feel to be a two-time champion, Hilton?"

"Were you worried when you missed those two long set shots?"

"Hold it, Hilton. One more please."

"Now you hand him the cup, Mr. Donley."

"That's right, Hilton, reach for it with your left hand and shake hands with the right. Good!"

When all the fanfare was over, Chip's pals ganged him, accompanied him to the locker room, and then embarked for Pete's Place where the real celebration began. Chip's teammates were there in toto with

Coach Corrigan and Henry Rockwell. The Statesmen and the Valley Falls crowd and the Tech stars and Pete and the State Drug staff were throwing a party in Chip's honor.

It was warm and friendly inside Pete's Place. Outside, it was cold and windy. There were a few pedestrians on the streets, hurrying along, anxious to gain shelter. But one man was in no hurry. Jim Locke stood at the end of one of the large windows of the restaurant watching the happy celebration inside. His sharp eyes registered each of the occupants and he paid particular attention to the joy of Chip's basketball teammates, the Statesmen.

Locke stood in the cold a long time, his brow furrowed, a puzzled expression on his face. "I must have had this kid all wrong," he muttered, turning away. "I've made a big mistake. Bill Bell is right." He pulled the collar of his overcoat up around his neck and walked slowly away, buried deeply in thought.

It was a real party. There was lots of food, good cheer, lots of basketball talk. Most of it concerned Chip's successful defense of his marksmanship title, but a lot of the talk was about the game with A. & M. and the effect a victory would have on Tech's tournament chances.

Chip was glad to get home when it was all over. The tension had broken with the victory and now the fatigue set in. He went to bed feeling as if he could stay there for a week. But, strangely, he couldn't sleep. When the first streak of dawn appeared, he dressed quietly and tiptoed softly out of the room. And when Soapy's alarm rang a half hour later, Chip was reading the papers.

"About time you woke up," he said. "Here, read Jim Locke's column."

"I thought you were going to stop reading that guy's stuff."

"Coming from you, that's good," Chip said, crossing the room to Soapy's desk. He pulled the drawer open and leafed through the clippings. "Are these yours?"

Soapy pulled the bedclothes up over his head. "Yeah," he said in muffled tones, "they're mine."

Chip opened the *Herald* to the sports section and read Bill Bell's column.

CHIP HILTON RETAINS HIS MARKSMANSHIP TITLE

A true champion retained his national marksmanship championship last night for the first time in the history of the tournament. Chip Hilton has been playing all season for the State varsity basketball team on a bad leg and wanted to withdraw from the tournament many times. But he was prevailed upon by this writer and a number of other interested persons to stick it out.

Unfortunately, there are certain prejudiced persons who are seemingly unaware of Hilton's contributions to State's athletic fortunes and teams without the benefit of an athletic scholarship. Hilton is working his way through school and ranks in the first ten in his class . . .

A picture of the Tech team caught Chip's eye and he studied the faces of the players. Immediately below was a list of their victims and the scores.

Chip glanced down the basketball score column and then shook Soapy's shoulder. "You can come out now, Soapy. I've got some real news. Southern took Western last night and that puts A. & M. in the championship spot."

"Temporarily," Soapy growled.

"So," Chip continued, "Western and Brandon have finished their seasons and are tied for second place with twenty wins and five losses, and A. & M. leads with a twenty and four record and with one game to play."

"It will be a three-way tie for first place after Monday," Soapy said confidently.

"If we can win tomorrow night," Chip said jubilantly, "Tech will have a chance for a berth in the N.C.A.A. tourney. A. & M., Western, and Brandon won't have time enough to play off the tie. Boy, I'm so nervous I can't sit still. I think I'll take a walk."

"In all this rain?"

"Sure. I like to walk in the rain. You had better get some more sleep. You and Biggie are on duty tonight. Remember?"

"Yeah, I remember," Soapy said sleepily. "What's my post?"

"You cover the Triangle and Biggie takes the City watch," Chip said, glancing out the window. "And it's going to be a tough night."

It was a tough night. The rain had turned to snow when Soapy and Biggie started out for their watches and Chip felt sorry for them. But he wasn't going to let anyone fall down on a watch. He studied until Biggie showed up at twelve o'clock to take over his night job as guardian of Jeff's heating plant.

"Anything happen?" Chip asked.

Biggie shook his head disgustedly. "Not a thing. But the guy was still open when I left. Well, I'd better get on the job or I'll get fired."

Chip studied a few minutes longer and then began to worry. It was past his training bedtime but he didn't intend to go to bed until Soapy came home. Ten minutes later he put on his coat and started out for the Triangle Service Station.

It was only a short hike and Chip chose the most direct route, a driveway which extended clear across the campus. He strode swiftly along, giving his knee no quarter. Long before he reached the watch post, he could see that the station's lights had been darkened. Chip debated his course of action and then started back to Jeff on one of the wide campus walks, hoping to overtake Soapy.

As he rounded a turn in the walk he was surprised to see a car up ahead blocking the walk. A man was standing near the rear of the car looking helplessly down at a flat tire. The soft, wet snow muffled Chip's steps and he cleared his throat so the man would not be surprised. "Can I give you a hand?" he asked.

The man whirled quickly about, startled and wary. As they stood there, appraising one another, Chip tried to see the man's face. But that was impossible. The stranger's hat brim was pulled down over his eyes and his coat collar was turned up around his neck.

"You can't help me," the man said gruffly, turning quickly away. "They're both flat. The spare, too. Of all the luck!" He looked up and down the path. "I've got to get one of these tires fixed. In a hurry!"

"The gas stations are probably all closed. I just came from the Triangle—"

The man pivoted quickly. "Was it closed?"

"Why, yes, it was."

"I was afraid of that."

"You might try the City. It stays open a little later. It's only seven or eight blocks from here. On the corner of Main and—"

"I know where it is," the man said shortly, turning away. Walking to the back of the car, he yanked the spare out of the trunk and started back along the walk, rolling the tire rapidly through the snow.

Chip walked slowly away, nettled by the man's abruptness and puzzled by the fact that the man had driven his car along a campus walk instead of using one of the regular driveways. The walk was wide enough to be mistaken for a driveway, but the man appeared to know exactly where he was and where he was going. Why hadn't he used a drive-way?

Then, in the distance, Chip heard a police car siren and glanced back. The man stopped, then turned and hurried back toward the car, rolling the tire swiftly before him.

Suddenly, on a hunch, Chip turned off the road and stepped into the shadow of a tree. He could barely make out the car, now. Then he heard the motor start and a second later, without lights, the car came bumping along the walk. After the car passed, Chip followed, keeping pace until the car was less than a block away from Jeff.

At the edge of the campus, the driver parked the car in the shadows beside the walk and cut across the lawn to the driveway exit.

Chip could see the man peering up and down the street. "He's afraid of being seen," Chip muttered.

He waited, his mind racing from one thought to another. Where was Soapy? A dark car with a light top . . . If he could only get a look at the license plate. "Well," he breathed, "what am I waiting for?"

He hurried toward the car, watching the man intently and keeping in the shadows. Reaching the rear of the car, he tried to read the license numbers. But it was too dark. Chip reached down and tried to feel the raised impressions of the numbers. Then something strange happened. Under the pressure of his fingers, the license plate swung upward until it was in a reversed position. And it remained there!

Chip whistled softly and walked swiftly around the car and tried the front plate. It did the same thing, swung upward, revealing only a blank surface. It required a determined tug to pull the plate down.

He glanced toward the gate again, and, at that instant, the man turned and started back to the car. Chip froze, caught in a moment of panic.

He waited for a tense, split second and then made a sudden decision. Creeping along the side of the car away from the approaching runner he opened the rear door of the car. As he crawled cautiously in on the floor of the car his hand encountered a blanket. "What a break," he breathed, pulling the blanket over his elongated form and crowding as far forward as possible.

Chip closed the door gently, holding the handle so it wouldn't swing open. "Now I'm in the soup," he breathed.

The running man's labored breathing was clearly audible now. He slid in behind the wheel and started the motor. The car moved slowly away, swaying slightly as it bumped along. When the driver reached the street, he clicked on the lights. Chip could now see the street-corner lights and wanted to peer out. But he was afraid to move. He watched for the street corners and figured the driver had covered no more than three blocks before he turned the car off the

street and proceeded up a rough lane. Now, the
street lights were dim and further apart.

Chip counted two turns to the right and one to
the left. Then, near a dim street light, the car slowed,
turned left again and stopped, and the driver got
out. Chip pulled himself up by the handle of the
door until he could see over the front seat. The
man was opening the door of a small garage. Chip
lowered himself and held his breath. If he was
caught now . . .

Then the man was back and drove the car into
the darkness of the garage. Chip waited, scarcely
breathing. Now what? . . .

The car's lights clicked off, leaving only the dim
reflection of the street light to illuminate the building. The man fumbled beneath the front seat and

*Chip pulled himself up until he could see
over the front seat*

got out of the car. Chip cautiously raised himself. The man walked toward the rear of the garage, barely visible in the dim light. Then he paused and took off his hat. After a second, he tossed the hat up on a high shelf and turned back. Chip ducked just in time to avoid discovery.

A moment later the garage door closed gently and Chip heard the click of a lock. The building was in total darkness now, and Chip slipped out of the car and moved slowly to a small window in the side of the garage. Next door was a two-story house.

As Chip watched, a light flashed on in a window on the second floor. Chip moved away from the window. What to do . . .

He tried the door but it wouldn't budge. Objects in the small building began to take shape and then the full implications of his position struck home. Here he was inside a building trying to get out . . . This was no joke. He was trespassing on someone's property, and if he forced his way out, he could be accused of breaking and entering. Or, rather, breaking out! Either way, it was trespassing.

Chip tried to figure out why he had followed his impulse to trail the man. He was thinking about the robberies, all right. But was he justified in going to such extremes? The man was worried, but that could have been due to the bad tires or because he was late or for any number of reasons. The fact that he had been aloof could have been due to his fear of a stranger. And lots of people had dark cars with white tops . . .

But what about the man's retreat to the car when he heard the police-car siren? Well, Chip reasoned, he may not have heard the siren. Or, he may have figured the City Service Station might be closed and have made a sudden decision to drive the short distance home on the flat tire. It could have been an old tire. . . . But why did the man run back to the car from the street? He certainly had acted suspiciously. . . .

"I'm wasting time," he breathed. "I've got to get out of here—in a hurry!"

CHAPTER 19

THE NICK OF TIME

THE reflected light from the second-floor window of the house suddenly disappeared and Chip returned to the window. The house was now in darkness and he tried to find a weakness in the window. He felt along the top and found two nails at each corner. They had been driven through the window frame and into the boards on each side. Both sides were nailed firm and tight.

Next, Chip tried the door. It was just as strong. He ran his fingers over the doorframe, hoping to find a weakness in the wood. But the boards were sturdy. Then he felt the bolts which held the hasp. The small nuts were screwed almost into the wood and it was impossible to move them.

"If only I had a wrench," he murmured.

He moved cautiously to the back of the building and found a workbench. Several wrenches and other tools were hung on the wall and he found one which he thought would fit the nuts on the door's bolts. Working feverishly with the wrench, he finally removed the nuts from the bolts. Then he pushed the door back and forth until he was able to force the bolts out through the holes and the hasp came free. Now he could open the door.

Chip pushed the door open and inched through the opening. The house was darkened and there was no one in sight. "What a break!" he whispered, hurrying away. "I'm lucky to get out of this."

Then he thought about Soapy and stopped short. He was getting out, all right, but he hadn't accomplished a thing. He could at least get the number of the license.

He slipped back into the garage and picked up the wrench. Working quickly, he removed the front plate and made his way out of the building and the short distance to the corner light. When he got there, he wrote the name of the street on a piece of paper and quickly copied the numbers from the license plate. Then he returned to the garage, closed the door, and replaced the plate. When Chip emerged from the garage, he didn't know whether he was in luck or in trouble. But he was going to find out. He had gone too far to back out now.

"I've got to call Lieutenant Byrnes," he told himself. "He'll know what to do."

Chip hurried back to Jeff. "Now to tell Soapy," he whispered excitedly, hurrying up the steps.

But Soapy's bed was untouched. Chip hesitated long enough to note that the clock showed two thirty and then he slipped quietly downstairs to the telephone booth.

Lieutenant Byrnes was sleepy and not too enthusiastic until he heard about Chip's adventure. Then his voice became brisk and his interest sharpened. "You might have something there, Chip," he said sharply. "In the nick of time, too."

"What do you mean, Lieutenant?"

"It's a long story. I'll be at Jeff in ten minutes, and then I'll tell you all about it."

Chip walked down to the basement and found Biggie dozing in front of Jeff's big furnace. "Biggie! Wake up! Have you seen Soapy?"

"No, Chip. Isn't he in bed?"

"No, and it doesn't look as if he's been home. He's never done this before. I'm worried."

"Where have *you* been? You're the one who ought to be in bed."

"I know. I'll tell you all about it when I get back. Lieutenant Byrnes is picking me up in a couple of minutes. If you see Soapy, tell him to wait right here with you until I get back."

Lieutenant Byrnes pulled up in front of Jeff just as Chip reached the door. On the way to the police station, Chip apologized for waking the officer and told him about his experiences of the evening.

"I don't know what made me get in the car, Lieutenant."

"It wasn't very smart, Chip. You might have gotten into serious trouble. Especially if he was the man we're after."

"Is there any way we can find out?"

"Perhaps. First, we've got to see Parks and Minton. By the way, I've got some bad news for you."

"Soapy?"

"That's right. The Triangle was held up again. A little after midnight."

"But Soapy was on watch. Right there."

"Parks and Minton figure differently. They arrived less than a minute after Welsh was robbed and they picked Smith up a couple of minutes later. And he was running. Running away at full speed. . . ."

Detective Fred Parks was annoyed. He strode back and forth in front of Soapy, shooting one question after another at the unhappy redhead. Gil Minton was sitting behind the table studying his notebook and Welsh was squirming uneasily on a chair opposite Soapy.

"I don't have any money," Soapy said firmly, "and I never had a gun and I didn't have anything to do with the holdup. When I saw Welsh lock up the pumps and turn out the lights I started for the hot-dog stand to get a sandwich."

"Why were you running?"

Soapy shook his head resignedly. "I told you. I run every day. I like to keep in shape."

The questioning was at a stalemate when Lieutenant Byrnes and Chip arrived at police headquarters.

Chip had seen his pal in a lot of tough situations during their many years of friendship, but he had never seen the redhead in such a sorry state. Soapy's face was scarlet and the freckles stood out like small blotches of red paint. Although the temperature of the room was a little on the cold side, perspiration was pouring down his cheeks. But he was full of fight.

"What's he doing here?" Parks asked, nodding his head toward Chip.

"I think he's got some information which may interest you," Byrnes replied softly.

"Oh, no!" Parks groaned. "Please—"

"He's got something that looks hot to me. You tell him, Chip."

Chip told about the car, the absence of lights, the flat tire, the presence of the car on a campus walk instead of a driveway, the license plates, and the man's strange actions when he heard the police-car siren. "And it was a dark car with a light top," he concluded, waiting expectantly.

"There was no car tonight," Parks said sharply. "The man was on foot."

"But couldn't he have left his car on the campus and walked to the Triangle?"

"That he could," Parks admitted. "However, you're overlooking an important point. We saw Smith running away from the station."

"What about the money?" Soapy demanded. "Welsh says the man took over a hundred dollars. If I had robbed him and was running away from the place, wouldn't I have the money?"

"You could have dropped it," Minton interrupted. "I—"

"Hold it, Gil," Byrnes said hastily. "I don't want to break in on your case, but a lot of things in Hilton's story add up."

"But what can we do?" Minton asked. "We can't wake a man up in the middle of the night and ask him if he's a robber just because Hilton says he was acting suspiciously."

"That's right," Parks added. "We can check the license number and get a search warrant in the morning."

Byrnes nodded. "I know. But that might be too late."

"Excuse me," Chip said. "Couldn't you take Mr. Welsh out there to look at the car?"

"So?" Parks said.

"Well," Chip continued, "if it's the same kind of a car the robber used in the other holdups, couldn't you wake up the man and tell him about the garage door?"

"And then," Parks prompted.

"Then, if Mr. Welsh recognizes the man, couldn't you arrest him?"

"I imagine we could," Parks said dryly. A brief smile flashed across his lips. "But you seem to have forgotten that Welsh has already identified Smith."

"But it hasn't been very convincing," Chip persisted.

Parks looked at Minton and waved his hands helplessly. "What do you say, Gil?"

"It's worth a try. We're not making much progress with Smith. What will we do with *him*?"

"Take him along," Byrnes said quickly.

Soapy gulped and looked at Chip. "Am I glad to see *you* . . ."

Lieutenant Byrnes led the way in his own car and Detective Minton drove the squad car with Soapy, Welsh, and Parks. Lieutenant Byrnes drove directly to the street and parked at the corner. Then they proceeded on foot to the garage. Inside, Minton and Parks focused their flashlights on the car and turned to Welsh.

"It looks like the car, all right," the station attendant said.

"So far, so good," Byrnes said.

"Maybe," Parks muttered. "Check the plates, Gil."

Detective Minton examined the rear plate, lifting it just as Chip had done. Then he moved to the front of the car and tried the forward plate. "Nothing much wrong, Fred," he said a moment later. "The plates have long bolts holding them to the frame and they *do* lift up— But that doesn't mean much."

"All right," Parks said impatiently, "come along. We'll soon know."

When they reached the porch, Parks waved them away from the door. "I'll do the talking."

Chip moved close to Soapy and elbowed him sharply. "This is it, Soapy!"

"Quiet!" Minton hissed. "Move back."

They grouped in the shadows while Parks pressed the doorbell several times. Seconds later, a hall light flashed on and a man peered out through the curtained window of the door. Then he turned on the porch light and opened the door. "What is it?" he asked sharply. "What do you want?"

"We're police officers," Parks said shortly, flashing his badge. "Can we talk to you?"

The man hesitated momentarily, cautiously eying Detective Parks and his companions. "Sure," he said reluctantly. "Step inside."

They filed into the small hallway and followed the man into the living room.

"Is this your man, Welsh?" Parks asked.

Welsh scrutinized the man carefully and shook his head. "I never saw him before in my life," he said confidently. "It's not the man."

"Well, that's that!" Parks said disgustedly.

"Just a second," Chip interrupted. "This man is too tall. The man driving the car was no taller than Soapy. He was built just like Soapy."

Parks checked him. "Just a second." He turned to the man. "Is that your car—the one in the garage next door?"

"No. It belongs to one of our roomers, Jim Beck."

"Is he here?"

"If the car is in the garage, he's here. Do you want me to call him?"

Parks nodded. "Yes, I do. I'll go with you. Gil, suppose you come along. The rest of you wait here."

Chip, Soapy, Lieutenant Byrnes, and Welsh waited impatiently as the officers and the house owner ascended the steps. After a short silence, there was a knock on a door. A muffled conversation followed. Chip was counting the seconds, his shoulder braced against Soapy. Then a well-built man, attired in trousers and a pajama top, appeared in the doorway of the living room. Parks and Minton pressed closely behind him.

Welsh leaped to his feet and pushed forward. "It looks like him," he said, puzzlement registering in his voice. "But he hasn't got red hair."

"What's this all about?" the man demanded aggressively. "Whaddaya mean wakin' me up in the middle of the night?"

"I'm sorry, mister," Parks said appeasingly. "We made a mistake."

They trooped down the steps and started back toward the cars parked at the corner. Behind them, the door slammed shut and the porch light was extinguished.

"Now, Hilton," Parks said icily, "I hope you'll stick to your books and games and let us handle the police department."

"What about the garage?" Minton asked. "We didn't tell him—"

"That's right!" Chip cried excitedly. "The garage! I forgot something. Wait! I'll be right back."

CHAPTER 20

THE FABULOUS FIVE

CHIP turned and dashed back up the street and through the open door of the garage. He edged through the darkness beside the car until he reached the rear of the building. Reaching up, he felt along the shelf and pulled down the bundle the driver had placed there. Even in the dark Chip could tell he was clutching a hat. Inside was a hairy object.

"A wig!" he cried exultantly, dashing out of the garage. At the corner he extended the hat toward Detective Parks. "It's a brown hat and here's a wig."

Welsh grabbed the wig out of Chip's hand. "Yah!" he gurgled excitedly. "And it's red! Lemme see that hat! This is it. There's the two feathers! Just like I said. It's him! It's him!"

"Could be, all right," Minton agreed.

Detective Parks nodded. "Yes, it sure could. We'd better ask our friend a few more questions."

They made their way back to the porch. The owner appeared almost as soon as the detective touched the bell. "Now what?" he demanded.

"We want to talk to your roomer again."

The man gestured up the steps. "You know where his room is . . ."

He watched Parks and Minton take the steps two at a time and turned to Lieutenant Byrnes. "Don't you fellows need some kind of a warrant to bust into a man's house like this?"

"But we didn't bust in," Lieutenant Byrnes said evenly. "You let us in."

"Sure. It was let you in or else—"

"Oh, I don't think it was that bad."

They were interrupted by descending steps, and through the open door Chip saw Detective Minton leading the way. The roomer and Detective Parks followed in that order.

"In here," Minton said, hooking a thumb toward the front room. They filed into the room and Lieutenant Byrnes motioned to Chip, Soapy, and Welsh to follow them. Then the familiar questioning began. It was the usual procedure, with Detective Parks shooting the questions one after another and Minton taking down the answers in the notebook.

"What's your name?"

"Jim Beck. Why?"

"Is this your hat?"

"Sure. It looks like my hat."

Parks held up the red wig. "This yours, too?"

"Yeah. So what?"

"Is that your car in the garage?"

"Yeah."

"Did you use it tonight?"

"Sure. I use it every night."

"Why?"

Beck shrugged his shoulders and repeated the question. "Why? Why to get home. I'm on the four-to-eleven shift out at Martin's."

"So you got off at eleven o'clock. Then what did you do?"

"I came straight home."

Parks dangled the wig in the air. "What do you use this for?"

"Oh, just for fun. Masquerades and things."

"Recognize anyone in this room?"

Beck looked blankly at the ring of faces and shook his head. "No. Don't know any of them."

Chip started to protest but Welsh beat him to it. "It's the same voice," he said. "Make him put on the wig and the hat."

"No, you don't!" the man cried, whirling toward the door.

But he wasn't fast enough. Gil Minton grabbed his shirt and pulled him back. "Wait a second, feller."

Minton pushed the suspect into a chair and turned to Parks. "Now what?"

"Think I'll have a little look at the room upstairs," Parks said, turning to the house owner. "Mind going along?"

The occupants of the living room waited quietly. All except Welsh. He put on quite a show. "I knew you all the time, Beck," he exulted, nodding his head vigorously. "You couldn't fool me. I was just waiting for you to make a false move."

"Oh, sure!" Soapy said significantly. "But you've forgotten something."

"What?"

"The blue sweater. Remember?"

Welsh nodded soberly. "That's right. Maybe he's not the man after all. But I'll know when I see him all dressed up. Brown hat, red wig, white face, and blue sweater. I guess I'd better tell those two detectives to look for that blue sweater."

"We won't need the sweater," Detective Parks said,

coming rapidly down the stairs. "I think we've got about all the evidence we need."

"What kind of evidence?" Welsh demanded.

"Marked money!" Parks said. "Lots of it." He turned to Soapy. "Well, Smith, this lets you out."

"Oh, boy!" Soapy said, grinning with his usual spontaneity. "I'm out before I'm in!"

"But it was close," Gil Minton said, putting his arm around Soapy's shoulders. "You're lucky to have such a persistent pal."

"And how!" Parks added. "Are you sure you're not studying criminology up at that college, Hilton?"

"Positive," Chip said, sighing with relief. "No more cops-and-robbers for me."

Minton laughed. "Good!" he said, turning to Soapy. "I guess you will find this hard to believe, Smith, but Fred and I felt sure all along that you were innocent."

"Even if we did give you a rough time," Parks said, grinning.

"It was rough, all right," Soapy agreed ruefully. Then the mischievousness was back in his eyes. "Say, Mr. Parks, did you ever study history, ever study about the Inquisitors?"

Parks shook his head. "Inquisitors? Never heard of them. Who are they?"

"Oh, just a bunch of people who lived five hundred years or so ago. You sure you never read about them?"

Parks grinned. "Maybe I ought to go back to school and study up on these—er—Inquisitors."

"Please don't!" Soapy said quickly, grimacing. "You know more about inquisitioning than they ever dreamed."

"Well," Parks said dryly, "if you're sure I couldn't learn anything—"

"I'm sure," Soapy said grimly. "Boy, you wrote the book!"

It was four o'clock when they got back to the police station. Jim Beck was booked immediately and placed in jail, and then Chip and Welsh signed statements for the record. While this was going on, Lieutenant Byrnes was on the telephone calling the *News* and *Herald*. Soapy listened in, a big smile spreading over his face from ear to ear.

When Chip and Soapy reached Jeff, it was nearly daylight on the morning of the big game of the year, the game against State's bitter rivals, A. & M. And Chip had broken every training rule in the book.

"Gosh, Chip," Soapy said worriedly, "if Corrigan finds out you were up all night, he'll throw the book at you. Throw you off the team."

"He won't have to find out," Chip said wearily. "I'll tell him myself. Tonight. Just before the game."

"You think you should play tonight?"

Chip nodded. "I'll play if he puts me in. It's up to the Coach."

"Boy, will the gang be surprised when they hear about the holdup! You know something—I'm not going to tell a soul. I just want to see their faces when they read about it in the papers."

"It won't be in the *News*. It's too late to meet the deadline."

"Heck with the *News*," Soapy said disgustedly. "Just so it's in the *Herald*."

"How are you going to keep all this secret until the paper comes out this afternoon?"

"I'll keep it. You won't tell, will you?"

Chip yawned and shook his head. "Don't worry about me. I've only got one class this morning and I've got three cuts coming. I'm going to use one of them and stay in bed until game time. Good night or good morning, whichever it is . . ."

Meanwhile, down at University's police headquarters, the story was released to the papers. As soon as Chip Hilton's name was mentioned, the night reporters of the *News* and the *Herald* called their respective sports editors. That accounted for the presence of Jim Locke and Bill Bell. Each listened avidly to the story.

Chip was absent when his pals gathered at Student Union for lunch. "See the *News?*" Biggie asked.

"And how!" Soapy said quickly. "Wait until Chip sees this!"

"Imagine Doc Terring writing to Locke," Speed said.

Biggie nodded. "And imagine Locke printing the letter!"

"Listen!" Soapy said, pulling a clipping out of his pocket. "I'll read it. 'To Mr. Jim Locke.'"

"Why don't you read Locke's preliminary paragraph?" Biggie asked.

"Good idea," Soapy said, starting again. "Listen!

"'This reporter is printing two letters which were received some time ago. They speak for themselves.' Now comes the letter.

"'As the University medical officer, I feel that it is my duty to advise you that Chip Hilton has been under my personal care since he was injured in the Clinton basketball tournament. Due to his great desire to prove his loyalty to State and to his teammates, Hilton has suffered intense physical pain every time he participated in a game.

"'Time and again it has been necessary for me to order him to the side lines, despite his persistent pleas that he be permitted to play. His devotion to the team and to the game of basketball has won the admiration of his fellow players and the writer. Signed: Michael M. Terring, M.D.'"

Soapy was beaming. "How about that?"

"How about this?" Fireball chimed in, poking his finger into the paper. "'Hilton's devotion to the university and the team has been an inspiration to all of us who were aware of his desire to help us win.'"

Fireball held the clipping up so the rest could see. "Look! That's signed by every player on the team. Look at their names: Markley, Thornhill, Gowdy, Reardon, Bollinger, Jimmy, and Speed, of course, and Reb Tucker and all the rest. Now wasn't that a nice thing to do."

"Wait until Chip sees Locke's column," Whitty said. "He won't believe his eyes."

"The heck with Locke," Soapy said. "Wait until you see the *Herald* this afternoon!"

"What about the *Herald?*" Speed demanded.

"Oh, nothing," Soapy said mysteriously.

"You holding something out on us?" Fireball growled.

"Maybe," Soapy said gleefully. "Well, I've got to go to work. See you all at the game tonight."

Two hours later practically everyone in University was reading the *Herald*, and the reason for Soapy's exuberance was there for all to see.

The issue of the *Herald* should have been called the "Chip Hilton Edition." Chip's picture was on the front page with a complete story of his part in the capture of the "Midnight Stick-up Phantom." And he was mentioned in practically every column of the sports section.

The front-page story caused a lot of talk around University, but the stories on the sports pages drew the most attention. Down at State Drug, Soapy, Mitzi, Fireball, Whitty, and Mr. Grayson each got a copy of the *Herald* and read the stories together.

"Bill Bell says State and Chip Hilton can put Tech in the N.C.A.A. tournament tonight," Fireball said elatedly. "Listen! 'If State can topple A. & M. to-night, the conference race will be thrown into a three-way tie between A. & M., Western, and Brandon, each with twenty victories and five defeats. Looking beyond this big *if,* your reporter talked with Mr. Dan Wright, chairman of the N.C.A.A. tournament selection committee, this morning and was advised that should State defeat A. & M. to-night, Tech would undoubtedly be chosen as this section's representative.'"

"I like this best of all," George Grayson said, reading aloud from the paper. "'State's entire student body will be pulling for a victory over A. & M. to-night, so that their local sports rivals will be invited to represent this section in the tournament.'"

"Say that again!" Whitty said happily.

"'And, continuing in this vein,'" Grayson read, stressing the words, "'every starter on Tech's fabulous five is on the Dean's honor list and—'

"Hey! Hold it! We're getting jammed up. We've got work to do. Oh, Soapy, be sure to take Chip something to eat this afternoon."

"Use my car," Mitzi added, smiling mischievously. "And don't have any more flat tires."

"Never again," Soapy said solemnly, rolling his eyes. "Never, never again!"

Chip was just getting up when Soapy arrived with the papers and a complete dinner with the compliments of Pete Thorp and Jimmy Lu Chung.

The redhead could barely conceal his excitement. "Read the papers," he said. "Read the *News* first."

"I'll eat first," Chip said, enjoying Soapy's impatience.

When he finished the food, Chip leisurely read the papers and dressed without comment. Soapy didn't get it.

"What's the matter, Chip? Gee, I thought you would be tickled pink."

"I am."

"But you haven't said a word."

"Do I have to say something, Soapy? I think it's swell. But right now I'm thinking only about the game tonight. It means everything."

Coach Jim Corrigan and Henry Rockwell were in the coach's office when Chip arrived at the gym that night. Corrigan saw him pass the door and charged after him. "Hey, Chip!" he cried. "Come here! We were just talking about you. I guess everybody's talking about you. How's your knee?"

"It's fine, Coach. I'd like to tell you about last night—"

"Forget about last night!" Corrigan interrupted. "You report to Murph and let Doc look at that knee."

Henry Rockwell slapped Chip on the back. "Right. That little infraction last night might just turn out to be the best break of the year."

"Especially for Soapy," Corrigan added.

"Then you know about—"

"About Soapy?" Corrigan interrupted. "Sure, Chip. Detective Byrnes is one of my best friends. Rock and I have been in on that little difficulty all along. But that can wait. Right now, you had better report to Murph Kelly. He's waiting for you."

As soon as Chip opened the dressing-room door he was ganged by his teammates. They circled him and roughed him up with enthusiastic affection.

"It's Sherlock Holmes himself!"

"Where's your cap and pipe?"

"Aw, you know he doesn't smoke!"

"How did you like Locke's write-up?"

"See our names? See what we said?"

"Yeah, Kid. Any time you want publicity, just see us."

"Tonight's the night, Chipper. This is the night we put Tech in the tournament. For you!"

Murph Kelly came pushing through the mob of players. "Come on, come on," he said roughly. "Chip's due for a little trip upstairs to see Doc Terring."

Kelly hustled Chip away from his teammates. "This may be the last game of the season, Chip, but it's not going to be *your* last game. Not if I can help it. Come on. We're going to see Terring."

Doc Terring examined Chip's knee thoroughly and carefully, testing the ligament with his finger tips as Murph Kelly flexed and then extended the leg. "It's coming along, Murph," he said gently. "Two or three weeks' rest and it will be as good as new."

"The game tonight means a lot to me, Doc," Chip said simply. "I'd like to help win it."

"I know, Chip. I'll talk to Coach Corrigan. We'll leave it this way. If you're needed badly toward the end of the game, I'll tell the Coach he can use you. But only for a couple of minutes." He glanced at Kelly and nodded significantly. "That's it, Murph."

CHAPTER 21

HISTORY CAN REPEAT

ALUMNI GYM was jammed that night. The fans had formed in long lines outside the big arena long before seven o'clock. And when the gates opened, they overwhelmed the ticket takers and flowed through like a rampaging flood. Chip could feel the tension in the dressing room. His teammates felt it, too. It was something they couldn't explain, something they could only feel.

The fans felt the same way. The Statesmen found that out when they came out on the court for their warm-up. There was a brief silence, and then the tension broke with a flood of cheers. Chip came last, trying to conceal the limp, but finding it hard to do so. Then the cheers became a thundering roar as the fans rose en masse to tell Chip Hilton how they felt about him.

The cheers came rolling down around Chip, Soapy, Corrigan, Rockwell, Murph Kelly, Doc Terring, Jimmy Lu Chung and all of the Statesmen, just as they had at Clinton when State clinched the Holiday Invitational Tournament.

And behind one of the press tables, Bill Bell was on his feet applauding, just as if he were a freshman and one of Chip Hilton's most rabid fans. Then Bell got one of the biggest shocks of his life. Someone tapped him on the shoulder. Bell turned and his eyes widened in shocked surprise. It was Jim Locke. . . .

But it was not the Jim Locke that Bill Bell knew. This man was almost a stranger. Locke's habitual sneer was gone. His eyes were level and sincere and steady, and he extended his hand with a gesture of humility. Then, despite the surprised stares of his colleagues—the other sports writers—Locke moved forward beside Bell and joined in the applause.

Then the game was under way and Bill Bell turned to say something to Locke. But what Bell saw in the eyes of the rival sports writer checked him and he changed his mind; he said what he had to say with a smile and a clasp of his hand. Words wouldn't have meant anything then, anyway.

The tumult continued unabated all through the game. A. & M. played brilliantly and won a share of the crowd's acclaim, but the fans were there to root the Statesmen to victory and they weren't going to settle for anything less. And time after time, the cheers came rolling down, "Put Tech in the tournament! Put Tech in the tournament!" "We want Hilton! We want Hilton!"

But Coach Corrigan was following Doc Terring's orders and Chip sat on the bench. At the half, A. & M. led 45 to 41. And they were still out in front at the end of the third quarter, 62 to 58. Coach Corrigan still made no move to put Chip in the game, despite the pleas and chants of the fans.

With three minutes left to play in the final quarter, State came battling back to tie the score at 79 to 79. Then the Farmers' great pivot star, Lloyd

Jenkins, scored on a jump shot to put A. & M. in the lead, 81 to 79, and Markley called for a time-out.

The fans really got into the act, then, stamping their feet and chanting in unison:

"We want Hilton! We want Hilton!"

Chip was leaning forward on the bench, every fiber of his being tensed and poised and waiting for Corrigan's nod. "Now," he breathed. "It's got to be now."

But Corrigan passed him up, shook his head indecisively, and beckoned to Gowdy. Then the fans really went berserk. Alumni Gym became a bedlam of deafening, ear-shattering sound which seemed strong enough to veritably lift the roof.

Time was in, now, with two minutes and forty seconds to play, and the big hand was speeding around the clock. The Statesmen were desperate— the big game was slipping away. They tightened up, failed to drive, and handled the ball as if it were loaded with dynamite. The A. & M. players sensed the indecisive play of the locals and pressed forward, forcing their rivals back toward the ten-second line. Then Markley called another time-out and Coach Corrigan turned toward the bench.

Chip was poised and waiting and was on his feet as soon as Coach Corrigan turned. But fast as he was, the reaction of the fans was faster. Their shouts of approval became one continuous roar. Coach Corrigan was talking excitedly in the huddle, but Chip didn't hear a thing he said.

Then he was out on the floor moving on two soda-straw legs over which he had no control. But Jimmy Lu Chung took care of that, hit him with a pass and cut in front of Chip's guard, setting up a perfect screen. Chip's confidence returned. He concentrated on the hoop and took the shot. The ball went up and out in a perfect arc and swished through the net. That brought down the house.

The score was tied now, 81 to 81, with a minute and ten seconds left to play. A. & M. took the ball out of bounds under their basket, and State hawked them all over the court. But the Statesmen were fearful of fouling and the Farmers had little trouble advancing past the ten-second line.

Chip could hear Soapy, Bill Sanders, Ed Henry, and Stew Wilson yelling:

"Come on, Chip! Come on, Chip! Get the ball! Get the ball!"

And then, strangely and suddenly, Chip felt that he had been through all this before.

"History *can* repeat itself," he breathed. "It's got to . . ."

Except for the uniforms, the faces, and the score, the situation was the same as it had been at Clinton in the final seconds of the championship game. Then, too, the score had been tied. And the great Southwestern team had held the ball then—had played for one shot—just as A. & M. was doing now.

Chip glanced at Jimmy and then at the clock. Jimmy had made the interception in the Southwestern game.

But A. & M. was playing it safe; they held the ball and watched the clock. And they kept the court open, were wary, and faked before every pass. Again Chip glanced at Jimmy. "It's up to you, Jimmy," he whispered. "Come on! Get the ball!"

And bounding from the rafters and from the walls, and rolling down and around the players on the floor came the giant echo of the crowd:

"Get the ball! Get the ball!"

Jimmy didn't seem to hear a thing, never looked at the ball, concentrated solely on his man, played a tight man-to-man defense.

Chip glanced at the clock. Twenty seconds to play! Now, A. & M. began to move, began to maneuver for the last shot. The shot which could mean the conference championship, the bid to the nationals . . .

Fifteen seconds . . . fourteen . . . thirteen . . . twelve . . . eleven . . . ten . . . nine . . .

Then it happened! Just as it had happened before. Just as it will happen again, time and time again, in this game of uncertainties, in this great game of basketball.

Jimmy shot forward like a flash of light, seemed to move even more swiftly than the ball, made a lightning stab at the leather as it flew toward Jenkins under the basket. It was a desperate thrust, a last-gasp try for the ball. Jimmy nearly did it! But not quite. His straining fingers deflected the flying sphere but not enough for control. The ball went spinning across the court . . . anybody's ball!

Every player on the floor, it seemed, dove for the ball. But it was Sky Bollinger who reached it first. Sky took off in a flying dive and his long arm swept the ball away from the scrambling mob. The ball was nearly out of bounds when Chip caught it up and cast a frantic glance at the clock. Four seconds!

Then Chip saw the flying form of Jimmy Lu Chung. Jimmy had kept on going. He was speeding far down the court. All alone!

Chip's reaction was automatic; a replica of many a lightning pass on the football field. He threw the ball straight for the basket, giving Jimmy the same kind of lead he would have given a speeding end.

The ball and Jimmy converged on the basket and the speeding little fellow barely made it, sprang high in the air and stabbed at the ball. A split second after his fingers twisted the ball, the game buzzer drilled through the roar of the crowd. Then, just as if someone had pulled a giant switch, the crowd roar ceased.

Chip pulled his body far to the left, trying to impart body english to the ball from all that distance. He saw that the spinning sphere was impossibly out of line for a perfect arc into the hoop. He groaned and started for the bench. "Overtime," he muttered, "overtime."

Then the ball kissed the glass backboard in the upper right-hand corner and went spinning to the left. Chip thought his eyes had tricked him. He stared unbelievably as the ball darted away from the transparent glass and went spinning through the hoop and into the net. The ball hesitated just a fraction of a second, taking a little swing in the net, before it swished on through and dropped to the floor.

Then from nowhere, right up out of the floor it seemed to Chip, his teammates and the fans were around him and lifted him to their shoulders. Chip twisted around and saw that Jimmy was caught up by another cheering throng of fans. Jimmy was yelling at him, a triumphant fist raised in the air.

Chip was almost deafened by the tremendous roar of the happy State fans as they yelled and cheered and applauded and tugged at him. But in spite of the turmoil, he heard Soapy and Bill Sanders and Ed Henry and Stew Wilson:

"Chip! You did it! You did it!"